Y0-CQN-727

# THE ENTOMBED MAN OF THULE

# THE ENTOMBED

*Stories by* GORDON WEAVER

Louisiana State University Press
BATON ROUGE

# MAN OF THULE

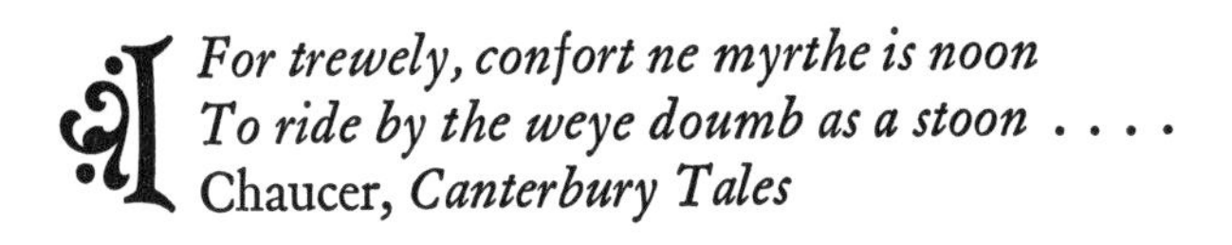

*For trewely, confort ne myrthe is noon*
*To ride by the weye doumb as a stoon . . . .*
Chaucer, *Canterbury Tales*

*For my wife, Judy, and our daughters, Kristina and Anna*
*And dedicated to the memory of my mother,*
*Inez Katherine Nelson Weaver*



ISBN 0-8071-0245-8
Library of Congress Catalog Card Number 70-185952

Manufactured in the United States of America
Printed by Vail-Ballou Press, Inc., Binghamton, New York
Designed by Dwight Agner

Some of the stories in this volume appeared originally, in somewhat different form, in the following publications: *The Fiddlehead, Confrontation, South Dakota Review, US Catholic, The North American Review, Perspective, the new renaissance, Prism international, Latitudes, Wascana Review, The Denver Quarterly.*

# CONTENTS

# FINCH THE SPASTIC SPEAKS

THE DOCTOR'S ACHIEVEMENTS with problems like mine are famous; his connection with the university—research and occasional lectures—accounts for my choice of this state, city, school. I had, of course, my pick of institutions. He is, I think, basically kind, but too great a scientist to obscure his ministrations with mercy or pity, and for this I am grateful. Though we have met each month for the past five years, we have no . . . what you would call *rapport.*

Answer a leading question: what is Finch? Is he the body, the badly made bundle of nerve ends and motor responses? Or is he the mind, the intelligence, the scholarships and fellowships, the heap of plaques, medallions, scrolls, given in testimony to his brilliance? Or is he something even more than these, a total greater than the sum of his parts? I ask you, does not Finch . . . feel?

Ah, you mock! Finch, you say, Finch of all people! Finch? Poor, pathetic Finch, with his tested and recorded intelligence quotient of two hundred and thirty-three, locked forever in his prison of chaotic muscles. Poor Finch, who falls as easily over a curbstone as an infant toddler over a toy. Unfortunate Finch, whose large, staring eyes often roll wildly behind his thick glasses. Tragic Finch, who must choke and strain like some strangling madman if he is to ask for so much as a drink of water.

You underestimate me.

Stripped to shorts and undershirt, I sit on the edge of the doctor's examination table, legs dangling. With an ordinary tape measure, he checks my calves, thighs, forearms, biceps, to see if any disparity has developed. Kneeling, he exerts pressure on each foot as I pull up against him, testing for any distinction in muscular strength. "Okey doke," he says, pausing to jot conclusions in the thick folder bearing my name that will doubtless one day yield monographs, to his ever-spreading renown. "Ready?" he says, handing pen and folder to the attentive nurse. I do not speak needlessly.

He stands near me, raises his hands, spreads his fingers like a wrestler coming to close with an opponent in the center of the ring. And I see it just that way, a contest, for my amusement. I am very strong.

Relaxation is the secret. I half-close my eyes to concentrate, bombarding my shoulders, arms, hands, fingers, with commands: relax! Gradually, the fingers twitch, release the edge of the table, and slowly my arms rise, fingers open to meet his. He meets me halfway, interlocks his fingers with mine, and we push, face to face. I watch his skin flush, eyes protrude ever so slightly, teeth clench. We push, as earnest as two fraternity boys arm wrestling for a pitcher of beer. I am very strong.

He grunts without meaning to, catches himself, pushes again, then gives up, exhales loudly. "Okay," he says. I smell the aroma of some candied lozenge on his breath. Is there a trace of sweat on his tanned brow? "Okay," he says, "okay now." To save time, the nurse helps him unlace our fingers.

There was an impressive formal reception when I came to the university, five years ago. Not for me alone, of course. Invited were perhaps a hundred new students with some claim to distinction: merit scholars, recipients of industrial science fellowships, national prize-winning essayists, valedictorians in great number. But, except for a small covey of timid and meticulous Negro boys and girls, to whom all the dignitaries paid solemn if perfunctory court, I was easily the center of attention.

Imagine Finch, the spastic, dressed for the occasion. (The habitual fraternity jacket was not to come until my sophomore year, when Delta Sigma Kappa, campus jocks, coming to know me from my work at the gymnasium, adopted me as something of a mascot, perhaps their social service project for the year—the jacket was free, as are the passes to football and basketball games. I could, if I cared to, sit on the players' bench.) I wear a dark suit with vest, and the dormitory housemother has tied a neat, hard little knot in my tie for me. I stand near the refreshment table, as erect as my balance will permit. My left arm is locked into place, palm up, whereon I place a napkin, a saucer, and a clear glass cup of red punch which I have no interest in tasting. With utmost care, I have tenderly grasped the cup's handle between thumb and forefinger, and there I stand, listening, questioning, answering, discussing (I speak extraordinarily well this day!) with a crowd of deans, departmental chairmen, senior professors, polite faculty wives, the president of the student body, and a handful of upper-class and graduate honor students. From time to time a few wander away to make a ritual obeisance to the Negroes, but they return.

Finch, Finch is the main attraction! Finch, with his certified intelligence quotient of two hundred and thirty-three, Finch who probes and reveals yawning gaps in the reading of graduate students ten years his senior, Finch who speaks with authority of science, literature, and contemporary politics, Finch who dares to contradict the holder of the endowed chair in history! Oh, there is glory in this! Finch, who cannot tie a shoelace, cannot safely strike a match, has trouble inserting dimes in vending machine slots—Finch is master here!

The other new students stand on the fringe of my audience, bewildered, or stroll off to stare dumbly at the obligatory portraits of past university presidents and trustees that dot the walls. I grow weary, but the tremor of my head can pass for judicious nodding, the tick in my cheek for chewing gum. The punch in my cup rocks a little. Who is the free man here?

Is it the scholar-professor who must think hard to recall specific points in his dissertation if he is to answer me? Is it the hatchet-faced, balding Dean of Letters and Science who carefully defends the university against its out-of-state rival, which also sought Finch? Is it the beautiful girl who won a regional science fair, but stands here, open-mouthed and silent as Finch explicates the relationship between set theory and symbolic logic? Is it the faculty wife with bleached hair, calculating her sitter's wages, who dares not depart for fear of offending Finch? Or is it Finch, whose brain roars with commands of discipline to his muscles, achieved only with the excruciating tenuous force of his will?

What you might think a disaster was actually the climax of my triumph. I had almost no warning. I felt the spasm that plunged my chin down against my chest, felt a stiffening come over my arms and hands, but no more. As nicely as if I wished it, I tossed my cup of punch up and back over my shoulder, while the saucer snapped in two in my left hand, giving me a rather nasty cut across the palm. There was a fine spray of punch in the air, the cup shattering harmlessly against the wainscotted wall behind me. Only the beautiful winner of the regional science fair forgot herself so far as to shriek as if she had been goosed.

I allowed no time for tension or embarrassment. I spoke

quickly, clear as a bell, "Please excuse me," and reached up with the napkin to wipe punch from my forehead and hair. I asked for a chair, was seated, and the conversation continued as before while my hand was bandaged.

Which of you, I ask, would dare such a thing outside your dreams? When I smiled they laughed. And the winner of the science fair blushed, mortified by her outburst, as I related other such experiences in my past for their entertainment.

Above all, do not underestimate me.

The doctor breathes heavily. At my sides, my hands still hold their clawlike, grappling shape. A small victory, I am stronger than he; something to savor for a short time each month. He writes again, says, "I trust you're keeping up with the schedule." I nod, or what passes for a nod. The nurse helps me into my shirt and trousers.

"I can't emphasize that enough, James," the doctor said. He has called me by my first name since I met him; I was, after all, only seventeen when my parents arranged the first consultation.

"I don't want to alarm you," he said, "but there is evidence of unilateral deterioration—" I know the jargon as well as he—"your right side's progressing fairly rapidly. I want you to stay with the schedule, and don't miss the medication. I'm going to write your folks . . ."

I have always kept the schedule. Ever since I can remember, there has been a schedule, exercises, work with weights, isometrics, special breathing and relaxation drills. At home, in my dormitory room, in classes, on regular visits to the gymnasium, I have faithfully kept the schedule. And medication. Pills, occasional injections as new serums and theories prevail. My wristwatch is equipped with a small but persistent buzzer to keep me precisely on the schedule.

"You know the literature on progression yourself . . ."

he is saying. The nurse is fastening the buckles on my shoes; I once counted it a great breakthrough to go from snaps to buckles. I looked forward to laces, but no longer care about such matters. The nurse brings my fraternity jacket.

"You do understand the import of what I'm saying, James?" the doctor said. I realized he wanted more than a nod or flutter of eyelids. I must speak.

I did not forget the beautiful winner of the regional science fair. I saw her now and again during my first quarter at the university. We passed in corridors, joined the same lines in the cafeteria and bookstore, and once, sat in the same aisle in the auditorium to watch a foreign film. Whether she seemed to notice me or not (how, I ask, does one *not notice* Finch?), I never forgot her face as I saw it when my hand was being bandaged at the reception, flushed with distress for her unmannerly and callous shriek at my misfortune with the punch cup. I understood she was emotionally in my debt until I should release her.

As these weeks passed, I began to pay attention, to sometimes go out of my way to meet her as she left a class or walked one of the narrow paths crossing the wide, green campus on her way to or from her domitory. I found stations, fixed and concealed points, from which to observe her at length. It was not until the first long vacation, however, that I recognized how affected I was by her beauty. Her name was Ellen.

Picture Finch: his father or mother drives him to the public library for a day's work, and he burrows into his books and three-by-five notecards with a determination the envy of any serious scholar. A librarian helps him carry books to a far, quiet corner near a window, where the sun's warm rays belie the frozen, cold stillness of the snow-covered streets and buildings outside. He begins, reads, writes, outlines, and time passes without his knowing it, or caring. But a dingy cloud throws him into shade, or the day has already faded to that dark, chill cast that is a deep winter afternoon. He lifts his trembling head, closes his eyes, sore with strain, and suddenly sees nothing, thinks of nothing, but the beautiful Ellen. History or political science or biology evaporate, and his reality consists only of her pale blond hair, the hazel tint of her bright, large eyes, the unbelievably fresh smoothness of her skin, the light downy hair on her arm, the sparkle of her white, even teeth; to the exclusion of even his lifelong awareness of his insane, spastic body, Finch knows only this beautiful Ellen!

I see, I *feel* the beauty of her movement: her hand glides to gesture, her fingers curl around a pencil, artless as the flow of water, no more self-conscious than the law of gravity; her head tilts, or she throws it to cast her hair back out of her eyes; she sits, crosses one long, sleek leg over the other, and it bobs in time to the animation of her conversation; she arches her back, thrusts out her breasts, and lets her coat slide down her stiffened arms as if they were greased rails; she climbs the steps to her dormitory, her knees churning like pistons, and pauses before the door to stomp snow from her high, black boots; alone on a path (but Finch, hidden, watches!) she holds her books against her stomach, runs, slides like a tightwire walker on a streak of silvery ice.

Ah, thinks Finch, oblivious to his books and the dry, clean smell of the library, *beauty!* She walks and runs, this beautiful Ellen, sits, jumps, with the floating, liquid perfection of some gaudy reptile.

It was Christmas, and I was home with my family, and I had reading and research papers to do, but I—why should I not say it—was in love. Finch was eighteen, and in love for the first time in his life. Yes, *Finch loves!* Or, thought he did. Loved, once.

"Jim?" says a voice outside this absorbing, warming reality

—it is his father, or his mother, come at the agreed hour. "Jim, it's time to go, we'll be late for supper." Finch opens his eyes, and it is winter again, cars make slushy noises outside the window, and he must reorder his mind, recall where he left off his research, stack his cards and papers, answer questions, think of real things, when and where and what he is.

It is Christmas Eve night, and my family gathers at the huge tree that dominates our living room. There are special things to eat, and I am allowed a little whiskey for the occasion. My mother is happy in her Christmas way, tears in her eyes as she hands me many expensive gifts, elaborately wrapped—a new fountain pen, made in Germany, with a thick barrel, so much easier for the fingers to circle; a cowhide briefcase with a manacle fitted to the handle so I can lock it to my wrist (this will require new feats of balance, but, to please her, I say nothing of it); an astrakhan hat, in vogue among students this year—she will not have me lack what others have!

I appear to enjoy this annual ceremony as much as they. I give, and get, an enthusiastic hug and kiss as I open each gift, being careful not to too badly smash or tear the fluffy bows and ribbons and bright paper as I unwrap each package, labeled, as always, *To Jim from Santa.* I faithfully follow my father's direction as he films all this, stooped behind his camera and tripod, his words just a bit thick with too much whiskey. I pose, seated on the floor between my younger brother and sister (they are both perfectly ordinary), put my arms around their necks, do my best to smile so that I will not look drunk or half-witted in the movie.

But I go to bed early, pleading fatigue, the ritual splash of whiskey, the research to be done even on Christmas day. I leave them, to seek Ellen, to be alone in my bed and nourish this thrilling, weakening sensation of love that for the first time in my life lets me, makes me, forget myself. My taut body relaxes in stages, by degrees, while my brain whirls gently with real and imaginary visions of this exquisite Ellen. I still hear music, the rattle of happy, sentimental talk as my parents sit up late, drinking and watching old Christmas films—and for the first time in my life, I am not ashamed of the erection that keeps me from sleep.

The good doctor has just informed me that my future is limited. The paralysis, unknown to me as I labor faithfully at my schedules, as I dose myself to the point of nausea, has been progressing. Subtle as a tiny worm, my malady has eaten away at this comic body, devouring days of my life. The figures noted in my folder already record the shrinkage from atrophy. The ultimate and sure end, if progression is not arrested, will be a spasm of sufficient duration, somewhere vital, the throat, the diaphragm, and I will suffocate in a final paroxysm, no different than if I had swallowed a fishbone. Yet he asks me to speak now, reassure him that I understand and face his diagnosis calmly.

He waits, brows lifted, expectant, needing; the nurse returns my file to the cabinet drawer. I speak, for us both, a lie.

"I'm . . . not . . . alarmed," I say, almost effortlessly. True, my mouth twists in shapes wholly unrelated to the words. My tongue emerges as I finish, and I am in danger of drooling idiotically, but the words, slow-paced, are only a little distorted, like the stridency in the voices of the deaf when they sing.

True, no one could take me for normal, but that I speak at all is a minor wonder.

"Good," the doctor said, "good," washing his hands. The nurse has left the room.

I have said, does not Finch feel? But feeling brings on

paralysis, interrupts the constant stream of impulses from brain to muscle—feeling means stasis, immobility. I must be alone if I am to allow myself grief or wonder. Solitude waits only on my tortured passage through the waiting room, a perilous descent of the stairs, a short ride on my bicycle to the dormitory.

Back at the university, I determined to call her. Though I might have known she would not refuse me, I shook as if I suffered Saint Vitus' dance, telephone receiver in hand, until she said yes, she would accompany me to a movie. "Will we be walking, Jimmy?" she asked. I faltered, choked, not having thought to the point of specific arrangements. Finch, pride of the history department, flustered like any juvenile! *No,* I managed to stammer: even the closest theater was a trek across the campus, far enough to be humiliating. I cringed, imagining us, arm in arm perhaps, floundering and swaying on the icy paths. "Oh," Ellen said, and waited for me to speak. I rocked fitfully on the small seat in the booth in the empty dormitory corridor. It might have sounded, in her ear, like the wild and frantic banging of someone prematurely buried.

I nearly mentioned my bicycle, but this was unsafe in winter for me alone—with her, perched on the handlebars, it would have been macabre. "I have a car, Jimmy," she said sweetly. And so we went in her car.

I do not remember what film we saw, for through most of the feature I sat rigid, inching my hand closer and closer to hers. Something happened in the film, something loud, action with bombastic musical accompaniment, and damning myself eternally a coward if I failed to act, at last, with a short, convulsive, clutching thrust, I slipped my hand over hers. She was kind enough to turn her head to me, and smile. We sat that way until the house lights came up, my sweaty palm covering the back of her smooth, cool hand. Surreptitiously, I breathed her delicious perfume, and from the corner of my eye, exulted in the delicate turn of her ear, her nostril, the way her blond hair swept upward on the back of her neck, the soft line of her throat, the faint heaving of her bosom.

We parked at the dormitory complex. It was very cold, and the other cars raised thick, steady clouds of exhaust. Their occupants, clasped in long, intense embraces, moved as shadows behind the frosted windows, all about us. Every few minutes, an engine died, a door opened, and a couple emerged to walk to one or another of the buildings. In the doorway lights we saw clearly their final kissing and fondling.

Ellen left the motor running, and we sat, silent. She wore a heavy coat, open, with a hood, a ring of snowy rabbit fur framing her face. We sat, quiet, while my brain raced, wondering what I should, or would, or could do. I did not want, at first, to touch her, but felt I must. I could feel the tick in my cheek grow worse, knew my limbs were frozen, hands balled in fists in my lap.

"Do you want me to walk with you to your dorm, Jimmy?" she said, and quickly, she leaned toward me, perhaps to open the door for me, I do not know. Somehow it terrified me, and I lurched, as if I had been given an electrical shock, and I spoke.

"No!" I said. I did not mean to touch her, not at first.

My left arm came up, swiftly enough to have given her a jarring slap, but stopped short, and I caressed her cheek and chin. She seemed to lean further toward me. I willed my right hand to take her shoulder and turn her fully toward me. I think she wanted me to kiss her, or thought I wanted to—I looked into her face, and she was, again, smiling, as she had in the theater. Her mouth was open slightly, her eyelids fluttering.

It was then I decided to kiss her, and let myself feel fully the love I had not permitted myself before, ever. I think I may have begun to cry.

I was not in love, I understand now, not in love with this beautiful Ellen, this precocious student of science, with her skin like milk, her grace of movement so inherent and unconscious as to put a dancer or an animal to shame. I did not love her, I say. I felt, then, as I moved my head closer to hers, the welling up of my response to all the love showered on me before, by my family, doctors, nurses, therapists, teachers.

Should not Finch, like you, feel?

I was, surely, crying, making a grotesque sound like the growling of a beast. I was moved by the collective force of all that love—my weepy mother, standing at the end of the parallel handrails, holding back her tears, whispering, *step Jimmy, step, one more step to mother, Jimmy;* my father, carrying me high on his shoulders in the teeth of a biting wind at a football game, cheering, *look at him go, Jimmy!,* suddenly letting me drop into his arms, hugging me to his chest, saying, *it's okay, Jim, it's okay,* because he thought I felt hurt, unable ever to run like that anonymous halfback; my teachers, *see, James knows, you're all so smart aleck, but James always has the right answer;* my sister, *Jimmy, are you the smartest person in the world?;* an auditorium filled with parents, the state superintendent of education saying, *I cannot say enough in praise of James Finch,* rolls of applause as I move, like some crippled insect, to the podium, everyone's eyes wet . . . I draw Ellen's face close to mine, my hand tightening on her shoulder. Stupidly, I try to speak.

*Kiss me,* I want to say, with all the force muted by all the tenderness of my need. And I am betrayed once more by my odious body. Ellen's mouth is closed to meet mine, and I gargle some ugly distortion of my intention: *Kwaryoup,* I say, and her eyes pop open in horror. I hold her tightly, feel her resistance, try again—*Keeeebryumbee!* erupts from my throat. She tries to release herself. *Sochavadeebow,* I am saying, trying to reassure her.

"Jimmy!" she says, and pulls at my wrists. "Let go, Jimmy!" I want to comply, but my left hand, nerves along my arm seeming to explode like a string of firecrackers, raises, comes down on her breast. "Jimmy!" she shrieks, and is crying now. "Get away from me, Jimmy, let go of me! Get your hands off me, you're hurting me, Jimmy!"

And it is over, mercifully. The door is open, I crawl or fall out, scramble through the snow on my hands and knees, slobbering, falling, thrashing. Behind me, I hear Ellen's nearly hysterical sobbing.

Ah, Finch, to think you might love! I no longer need to remember this, but when I do, am amused, recalling fairy tales of frogs and princesses, recited, sometimes hour after hour, in an effort to relax me for sleep, by my patient mother. A student of history, I remind myself, should have known better.

No matter. Before the following year was out, I had ceased avoiding her. When we meet now, we can even smile, though we do not speak.

As I leave, other patients in the waiting room pretend not to see me. An old woman with a cane and a platform shoe covers her eyes with a magazine. A palsied man, no more than forty, looks down at his shuddering hands. Another woman, younger, with a perfectly healthy looking child on her lap, suddenly becomes interested in her son's hair, like a grooming, lice- and salt-seeking primate. Yet another woman, her face set in a lopsided grimace, one shoulder permanently higher than the other, merely yawns, closes her eyes, pinches the bridge of her nose between two fingers until I am beyond her, as if she cannot bear her affliction so long as I am before her to remind her of it.

I walk to the door. I stagger like an old wino, head whipping from side to side with the thrust of each leg, as if I keep time to some raucous, private music. My arms are cocked, ready to catch me if I slip. My feet point inward, and my torso tips forward to provide the continuity of momentum, my broad shoulders thrown back to maintain a risky balance.

It is a gait to embarrass, to make children laugh, a clumsy cantering locomotion that results from only the most exacting and determined attention to control. Inside my rolling head, behind my shocked, magnified eyeballs, my brain orders, with utmost precision, each awkward jerk of thigh, leg, foot. Just as I reach the door to the stairs, a voice greets me cheerfully.

"Hello, Jimmy," sings out in a lilting feminine rush of genuine delight. I bang loudly against the door as I stop, gripping the knob with both hands for support. My head nearly hits the panel of thick, opaque glass. I turn with difficulty. "Hello, Jimmy," she says again.

I know her, but not well. She is a disgusting thing to see, a fellow-student. Fat of face and body, her legs are little more than pale pink, waxy skin stretched over bone, her feet strapped to the steel platform of her wheelchair. One arm is horribly withered, the thin, useless fingers held curled in her broad lap. The other is braced for strength to allow her to work the levers that steer her chair. Beneath her seat squats a large, black battery, her source of power. Her neck angles slightly to one side. Someone has recently given her jet black hair a hideous pixie cut.

I know her. She is one of the small, cohesive platoon of handicapped, crippled, maimed university students. They have an association of sorts, advised by a conscientious faculty member who lost an eye in Korea. The university provides a specially equipped Volkswagen van to take them about campus. They have keys to operate freight elevators, and the buildings have ramps to accommodate them. When I came to the university I was invited, by the one-eyed professor, to join their ranks. I even attended one meeting—mostly polio victims and amputees. The agenda was devoted to a discussion of whether or not to extend membership to an albino girl whose eyesight was so bad she could not read mimeographed class handouts. I declined to join, of course, but still receive their randomly published newsletter. We have nothing in common.

She smiles now, lipstick and powder, rouge and eyebrow pencil making a theater mask of her face. "I've never seen you up here before, Jimmy, have you just started coming?" I am struck, suddenly with the awareness that she has an . . . an *interest* in me! I grope frantically to open the door.

I must, and do, speak, but badly, without thinking, so shaken am I with my understanding. *Haroyoup* comes groaning from my lips, like the creaking of a heavy casket lid. Startled and embarrassed, she smiles all the harder, and I push open the door to begin the slow descent of the steep stairs leading to the street where my bicycle waits. Mad Finch, who dared to think he might feel!

At the top of the stairs I turn around, for I must descend backwards. I take the rail with both hands, regulate my breathing, concentrate, then step back, into the air, with one foot . . . I have a special sense of freedom, for I can never know if the foot will find the stair just below, or if I will step backward into space, find nothing, and fall. I am, for an instant, like a blindfolded highdiver who steps off the springboard, uncertain if there is water below.

I am able, momentarily at least, to forget my self-pity in this kind of freedom only I know.

I must not despair! Though Finch wields the chalk no better than a child does a crayon, he cuts surely as a surgeon to the heart of the problem on the blackboard. Though his pronunciation is atrocious, his syntax is exact, his structure flawless, vocabulary well beyond his years. Though his eyes, enlarged behind thick lenses, stare, sometimes roll up in his head, no one reads more or faster, and for amusement he will commit a paragraph or a page to memory in record time.

It is Finch who is free to traverse the lines of caste and class in our community. Finch is the locker room pet of brainless athletes. They challenge him to feats of strength, and lose goodnaturedly. From the heights of their chickenwire and toilet paper float thrones, Junoesque sorority queens wave to Finch in the crowd, call him by name. Filthy and morose, the bearded politicals and bohemians, who lurk in the basement of the student union, will take time to read Finch their latest throwaway or poem. Serious students, praying for futures in government or academia, consult Finch before submitting seminar reports.

Oh, I am not lonely!

So, with an effort of will, informed by the discipline of my regimen in physical therapy, weightlifting, my schedules, I heave, lifting my center of balance upward with an exaggerated shrug of my broad, strong shoulders; then, at the exact moment, a second divided into several parts for precision, I lean to the right, forcing all my weight onto my right leg, onto the raised pedal of my bicycle. There is no continuity, no fluid evolving process of motion, but my timing is correct—my mind has once more concentrated this fool's body into a preconceived pattern—the pedal depresses, the bike rolls forward.

There is an instant when disaster is possible—I am thrown forward with the bike, but my locked left hand grips the handlebar, stops me short of an ignominious and bruising tumble to the pavement. I remember to pull with my right arm, to isolate the individual muscles that will steer out, away from the curb, past the hulk of a parked florist's truck.

I move. Out now, near the center line, I assert the series of stiff, dramatic thrusts of hip and leg that pump me along, past the campus shops, the bus stop.

Students throng the sidewalk, and they call to me. The frat boys, the unmercifully attractive girls, golden and creamy in their expensive clothes, jocks in their letter sweaters and windbreakers, malcontents in old military jackets. They call: "Ho Finch!" "Jimbo!" "Hi Jimmy!" They grin, wave. "Baby Jim boy!" "Hi Jim," they call.

With careful, paced breathing, I multiply the complexity of my ordeal. Almost one by one, I unlock my fingers from the handlebar. With the strained deliberation of a weight-lifter, I raise it above my head, steering and balance both entrusted to my left arm. Aloft, the tingling spasms are sufficient to produce a casual wave. Like a swimmer shaking water from his inner ear, I rock my head, once, twice, three times, until I face them. Opening my jaw is enough to pull my lips back over my teeth: a smile.

In this instant I am helpless. Were a car to swerve into my path, a pedestrian dart in front of me, all would end in an absurd, theatrical collision—perhaps serious injury. But I prevail.

Now, the breeze in my ears, my glasses vibrating on the

bridge of my nose, threatening to fall across my mouth, I speak. My tongue bucks and floats, the stiff planes of my throat shiver, and I respond.

"Jimmy!" they cry. "How you doing, Jimbo!"

*Hyaroul* explodes my voice, and I can almost see their delight, the fullness of quick and easy tears of sentimental pity form in their eyes. *Hyarouffa!* I say, already plotting how I will lower my right hand, face the road again. *Haluff!* I make of unexpelled breath, not knowing if it is my cry of joy at being alive, known, loved, or a curse far more terrible than any profane cliché they will ever know—because . . . I suspect . . . simply because I cannot answer my own questions, cannot know what is, or is not, Finch.

# PORCH FIXING

THOUGH IT WAS LATE, Harrison began a letter to his brother. He found paper and envelopes in a desk drawer under the dusty Gideon Bible. Across the asphalt court there was a bar with its windows open, the sound of quick music and a sporadic female laugh, but if he slept or drank or whored, the next morning would leave him time and inspiration for only the cryptic phrases allowed by the dimensions of a postcard.

*Dear Howard, Nadine, and All* he began, then stopped to wonder who he meant by *All.* Howard had only one son, and Richie no longer lived at home. Surely Nadine passed family news on to her only child, but beyond that, who? Who did he mean? Harrison closed his eyes for a moment to address himself to everyone and anyone who had ever brushed against or collided with, escaped or evaded, tricked or trapped him.

At first he wrote rapidly.

*You'll have to surmise much brother mine because there are questions in your last letter (sent to Morgantown) that I must settle here and now. Briefly yes I'm well. This place is no Ritz but I know how to be comfortable in motels. Yes I'm in California, yes I've crossed continent again in search of employment, which explains the scenic postcard I sent from Phoenix. I've left Morgantown for good and all as al-*

*ways and yes I know I must stick fast somewhere but what else is education for if not to develop versatility? I adapt, Howard. Wish me luck. I'll explain all later.*

Music and the woman's laugh came across the shadowed court, but there was no time. If he walked out he would never get to it, ever.

*In your last letter you seemed thinking I nursed spite because everything of mother's was yours when she left us. No, Howard. No. I had my pick of keepsakes, so what more did I need. The house then. Because she left the house to you. No Howard. I live in motels. I never wanted it, actively I never wanted it. The only thing bothers me was the porch. Do you remember fixing the porch for her, Howard?*

Harrison remembered perfectly. A liar needs a good memory. The porch fixing, that was 1948. That was the year of many letters between him and his mother. That was the year Truman made a fool of the Chicago *Tribune*'s headline, but that was in November, after the porch. That year he worked for Vulcanized Rubber Products, Inc., of Buffalo, New York. *Remember I came home in August,* he wrote Howard. Because at the end of July he called in sick a Friday morning and drove to New York City, a blind date arranged by a friend, tickets to *Mister Roberts,* calling in Monday sick, too, still in the city, but the girl in personnel recognized a long-distance call, the beginning of the end at Vulcanized Rubber Products.

Liar's memory: To this day he could fill out a job application complete to the lies under the reasons-for-leaving-last-position column without notes, and rarely could an employment interviewer spot him for a perpetual floater. Memory. *She wanted us to rebuild the porch for her Howard.*

He had not been gone long enough for the neighborhood to begin shrinking on him. But in a couple of years' absence it had begun to decline, as his mother complained in those letters to Buffalo. The house next door—*on the right as you faced our house Howard*—a sturdy brick, had been converted into a nursing home for old men, most of them county relief cases. His mother didn't mind that so much. "Poor things," she wrote to Buffalo, "they have nothing to do all day but sit on the porch. They just seem to shine when I say hello to them when I come home in the evening." But the street in front of the house had lost its priority by then, the winter's frost-gouged potholes still not repaired by the city; the sidewalks were cracked, and thistles grew in the cracks.

New types moved into the block. *Remember the divorcee Howard? Stacked, the one who paraded out every day about the time you got home from summer school.* His mother referred to her as the grass widow. She rented the house on the other side of theirs. In the morning she turned her four children loose. About the time Howard returned from teaching ninth-grade math to dumb-dumbs and flunk-outs (it took summer school to keep body and soul, because in those days teachers' salaries were a national disgrace), she waltzed down the front steps in her bathing suit, broad sunburned back glistening with oil. And was there also a Sicilian who left his produce truck right at the curb down the block all afternoon and evening? Harrison's mother would have felt the same about him if he'd been an organ grinder tethering his monkey on the lawn to graze.

She took Howard and him on a short guided tour of the large porch to indicate the extent of necessary repairs. She wore a housecoat, had interrupted her Saturday cleaning, but Howard wore good clothes to show he meant to do no work that day. It was afternoon, and the smell of brandy on Howard's breath was sweet as flowers. The old men sat on their brick porch watching them with empty eyes, and on the grass widow's porch her brood, with Howard's son, was playing loudly.

Their mother preceded them and pointed out salient features with the tip of her finger. When he looked close at her hands he saw nets of tiny lines and cracks, housework fingers, darning fingers, librarian's fingers, a lifetime of work without faith in handcreams. She ticked off the jobs quickly, and as she progressed, the achievement in her voice bloomed, as though saying were doing, and she wished even the old men and the grass widow's mob to know how much had been done. "Look there," she said. "That last column doesn't even support the roof. Step back here so you can see how the roof tilts. See that? You need to replace the columns. Now, here, come here and look close at this." And they followed her to the cement block foundation under one of the columns. "The mortar's crumbling out of the seams. You stick the garden hose nozzle in there and you can wash all that old mortar out. You'll need to replace that. Here, look what those damn kids have done."

The grass widow's children, Richie too, had kicked out a few of the loose slats so they could crawl in under the porch. Richie was six then? Seven? "They crawl under there in all that filth for club meetings or what-not," she said. "I want that fixed. First, though, you've got to crawl in there, one of you, and make sure the bracing is tight under the floorboards. That floor sinks inches when you step in the wrong place."

"I'll have to do that," Harrison said. "Howie's too big for that work." How many years had he lived under the assumption that someday he'd grow up to Howard's size?

"Look up there at the paint under the eaves," she said. "That's got to be scraped and sanded before you paint it or you might as well not do it at all." And how clear it was in her voice that she never remotely considered not-doing! There were people whose lives set unbreakable patterns for them.

"I don't see why we couldn't have this out of the way in a couple of weeks, working afternoons and evenings," he said, eager to please her, and because saying it was, somehow, proof they would do it.

"More work than you think, buster," Howard said.

She went on, projecting what should come later, her ideas dividing, multiplying. "The children have ruined the lawn . . . spade it up and reseed with perennial . . . sod for the strip along the porch, and a five-foot fence to keep them from running wild-Indian over it . . . on the other side I'm going to plant flowers . . . it's got to be done now or the whole shooting match goes to an eyesore and it's too late to save it."

Two or three times, he remembered, she looked over her shoulder, down the street, her face frightened like some nervous animal scenting a predator, as if from far down the block she sensed the approach of some gray, shabby spirit that wormed into the beams of houses to hollow and sag them, burrowed under lawns and parched them, embraced whole neighborhoods and generations to age them in its clasp.

"Two weeks," Harrison said to comfort her. "At most three." Howard snorted lightly, cleared his throat derisively, and walked sway-backed, hands-on-hips, to spit expertly into the gutter.

"Howard?" called his wife from the roof of the porch. She had climbed through a window in their upstairs flat to inspect the metal sheeting for corrosion. "This doesn't look so bad. It needs some patching and paint is all." Nadine had been infected by their mother's plans, now envisioned the porch roof, with lounge chairs and umbrella table, a solarium.

"Get down from there," Howard yelled at her. "The whole thing'll collapse under you if you don't watch it."

"Dirt," said Harrison's mother, brushing hair back from her forehead—he noticed graying now—"you fight it all your life, and when you die they throw it in your face." She climbed the steps to the porch to get a broom and sweep the front walk.

*Do you think she feared old age and death Howard? You know I knew the house would be yours. Yes she wrote about that after that spring, and about dying, because the two were connected for her.* If there were anything he could blame Howard for it would be that. How she had to nag him all year to get him started. *I don't blame you Howard.*

"You have to light a fire under your brother to get him to do anything," she wrote to Buffalo. She couldn't understand that, because the house, she wrote, was going to be Howard's, free and clear someday. She didn't understand a man who didn't at least take pride in his own home. Her half-interest was unrecorded; it was already Howard's on paper. That had all been worked out during the war when their father died, while Howard was in service and Harrison was in college in the A.S.T.P. program.

By the next spring, Howard had no choice; Nadine agreed with her, Harrison agreed with her. He sent Howard a postcard from Times Square. *Hi,* he wrote, *On my way to see Mister Roberts. Love to All.* And by the time Harrison left Vulcanized Rubber Products, with bitterness on both sides, it could not be postponed any longer.

Was it the drinking alone that did it? It only helped. Howard had gone on the wagon, as Harrison would stop someday, when like Howard he got next to age fifty and had suffered periodic bleeding ulcers. The drinking was only a means for breaking rhythm. Good work, work of proportion required rhythm.

Once, not so far back in the race, the family must have been comfortable with tools close by. His grandfather had been a farmer in Indiana, hardy immigrant Dutchman by the evidence of gray-brown photographs, and bending over to sort through the tools, Harrison remembered his father hanging a picture hook in the dining room and cursing because the nail would not drive straight.

*What have you done with all those tools all these years?* he wrote. They seemed to fit the hollows of his hands there in the cellar, imparting confidence, a mild faith that he knew their uses and care. A ripsaw for slashing through the grains of seasoned pine, a carpenter's rule that made him want to measure the depths and times of the old house, to know it as well as its builders had. A crowbar, cold as the skin of a snake.

"We've got enough to go in business for ourselves if we want," Harrison said.

"Most of this stuff is junk," his brother said, and so it probably was. The thing to do, if a man had children, that kind of thing, was to put some tools, pair of pliers or blunt-edge file, in the infant's crib, as Bob Feller's father was supposed to have given his son a baseball to teethe on. But that was Howard, large and capable enough in his studied apathy to deflate the enthusiasm of feckless men.

He was tall enough to slouch attractively, and his overweight, when he was younger, only increased the impression of his bulk. He squinted and frowned much, cutting permanent lines suggesting profoundly cynical speculation. He spoke in rumbling deep tones far back in his throat, carrying certain conviction; expressions of doubt and disbelief were rich in finality. He laughed sharply through his nose, dropped his chin slightly to smirk, and . . . well, how was a man to proceed under this? They never developed the rhythm that does good work of some magnitude.

*I wonder Howard that you never in your life doubted yourself.* Or was it only that he had never believed at all? He couldn't ask his brother a thing like that. Certainly not in a letter.

Summer school was over at noon; with generous allotment of time, Howard should have been home by half-past, but never came before one o'clock, sometimes two, even three, in the afternoon.

Although the heat was terrific that late August, demoralizing, enervating, his brother sat for minutes in his '41 Plymouth after he'd stopped in front of the house. Inside the car he sat sweltering with his head canted, listening to the engine before shutting off the ignition and getting out slowly, tie off and jacket over one arm. Often just then the grass widow would be leaving for the beach, so Harrison and his brother shared a lusting, lip-bitten view of her oily bare back as she high-heeled arrogantly to her coupe, carrying towel and picnic basket and magazines.

Howard stood at the foot of the porch steps, hands-on-hips, paunch pushing out his white shirt, glowering at the porch. Nothing Harrison said was ever right.

"I've got a head start on you," or "You're late," or when the frustration of his brother's indifference finally touched off anger in him, "Where the hell have you been? I can't jack up the roof and knock out these pillars by myself, can I?"

"I stopped off," he answered, or often only, "So?" And he was left to wait on the porch, perspiration standing out on his face and neck, feeling foolishly dressed in a set of

Howard's old army fatigues while his brother went upstairs to change his clothes.

Emergencies arose as they worked, things needed immediately, requiring a trip to the hardware store. "I'll run over to the hardware and pick up a cheap level," Howard said, "and if they want two fingers off my left hand for it, I can stop and borrow one from a guy I know hangs around the Elbow Room. Take a break. Maybe Nadine's got something cold to drink," he'd say, and leave in the Plymouth.

"What the hell kept you?" he would ask when Howard at last returned.

"I had to go damn near across town," or if he didn't care enough that day to lie, "I stopped off. Didn't you get a beer from Nadine? The refrigerator's full of beer upstairs." And the brandy on Howard's breath was light-sugary in the still, warm air. *We never developed rhythm, Howard. Watch ditchdiggers sometime. They do it with rhythm.* Nowadays they dug ditches, graves for example, with machines; the machine's rhythm never flagged.

Rebuilding a porch began at the foundation.

He crawled in there because Howard was too large. Howard passed in a hammer, and he wedged the four-by-fours in with delicate taps. He held them tightly in place with both hands for security while Howard nailed them with spikes from above, his hammer blows making the close, hot blackness shake with regular tremors, shower dust over his shoulders and into his hair. Clenching his jaws and eyelids shut only made it feel that the blows were struck off from within his eyeballs or next to the nerves of his molars.

He crawled out to blink at the sun, sense his skin running with sweat, the ninety-degree August heat like a tingling cold bath. From the prolonged cramping under the porch, his joints ached and his muscles shook with spasms. His fingers twitched when he tried to light a match for a smoke. "Jesus Christ!" he said to Howard as he stretched and kneaded the small of his back with his knuckles. But there was something to climbing up on the porch and testing the spring of the boards, to find them firm. Solid. By God, solid!

When the columns had been replaced and he was working on the eaves, it was early September and nearly time for Howard to begin teaching full-time again. Harrison had begun receiving referrals from a professional employment agency in Detroit. He told small lies to his mother when she asked how soon she could expect the porch to be done. He tried to push himself, and Howard too, but could not. He lacked . . . what? He still couldn't say, not to save his soul.

When he came out onto the porch at noon, figuring to get set up for an afternoon's work, selecting tools and materials, he looked across into the vacant eyes of two or three of the old men sitting on the brick porch of the nursing home next door.

"Good morning," he called to them, and back came two or three growls like the warnings of old toothless dogs fearful their places beside the stove were in danger. Watched, he felt he had to do something, show purpose, skill, prove himself in this element. Sometimes he retreated inside, suspecting bitterly that the old men, wise with idle days on their porch, combing the work experiences of lifetimes, had considered, judged, and condemned him.

While Howard mixed cement in a bucket to mortar the seams in the foundation below, he did the ladder work. He scraped and sanded and painted, and when he looked around to exercise a kink out of his neck, the two or three pairs of eyes, blank and accusatory as those of blind prophets, were waiting for him, glistening, rheumy. Compelled to speak, he said, "How's it going?" or "How's she look to you?" Again, the rattling growls: not bad, not good.

"What?" Howard called up, his hands coated with a plaster of wet and drying cement.

"I was talking to my audience here," and Howard looked at the old men, the old men at Howard; they all looked up at him. What was there to do but grip the sanding block a little tighter and stroke swiftly away at the old paint, sure he had been again measured by his brother and a band of crafty, half-minded old men, and been found wanting? *I was looking for satisfaction Howard.*

The children were worst when they ignored him. They played always at some game of great action, violence, noise, on the grass widow's porch. They distracted him from his work because they were so free of it. Children, he swore, have the best of it. The earth could split down the middle and children would play along the margins of the two cliffs. An ambulance could scream up to the nursing home, light flashing, carry off the husk of the dying or dead, and they stopped play to watch, but only because of the noise, red light, the attendants in uniform. They played at police, at fire, at death, always with noise and laughter. They left him alone, irrelevant.

The scraper squealed against the uneven wood, speckling his face with dime-sized flakes of old paint. It was awkward, and his forearm and shoulder soon ached from reaching up over his head to do the underside of the rain gutter. The wire brush made a noise like finger nails on a blackboard. Sanding powdered his skin with paint dust that stuck, stung his eyes, and itched as he began to sweat. He did it again and again, conscious, deliberate, defying the ladder that seemed to sway in the imperceptible breeze, a metal clamp patching a partial split in one rung. A crick dug into his neck, the deep bone ache ate into his insteps from the pressure of the ladder rungs. He had to pull at the air with his lips for thick warm breaths, and when finally he looked down, found only the eyes of the near-mad old men, carelessly condemning him, the children playing, oblivious of him.

He enjoyed fantasies of being a monk in a damp cell, a lifer in the state prison, a hobo walking on a deserted highway.

Yet he and Howard did get things done, lots of things, and there were moments when he, fresh from the bathtub, could look at the porch as if it were a bulky beast he'd thrown and bound.

The last day, the last good day, was after Howard had started the fall semester. It was only a couple of weeks before he had the interview that led to the job with J. I. Case in Davenport, Iowa; that was the first job he held less than a year—memory was a wonderful thing, Harrison thought. That day they were to cut up the old porch railings.

Once upon a time they really knew how to make porch railings! Solid. They were solid, three and a half feet high, wide planks tongue-in-grooved to two parallel four-inch rails, and artistic, the whole of it planed and chisled into Victorian geometrics of some kind. They were toenailed to the porch. With the rented saw they cut the lengths running between each pair of columns into halves, pried them out with the crowbar, heaped the sections in the yard behind the porch.

"If you cut that mess into small enough chunks we could have them to burn in the fireplaces," their mother said. She complained of being cold in winter in the house. They began to cut the railings into kindling, taking turns, one operating the saw, the other feeding the broad slabs, bristling with rusted nails that caught and snagged when pulled off the pile, over a makeshift sawhorse.

The gasoline chain saw belched exhaust and roared, bringing Richie, the grass widow's gang. On the porch, Nadine and their mother stood in the shade and quietly admired. The old men lurked at windows in the nursing home.

Though the blade was supposed to be freshly sharpened, Harrison had to lean his weight against it to cut through, then pull quickly just as the cut was finished to keep his momentum from bringing the chain blade against his leg; a man's bone and muscle might be severed instantly. When Howard was doing the sawing, he cursed incessantly, showed his teeth, and set the saw down frequently to wipe his face.

When he sawed he worried that Howard thought he was too slow, would walk off in disgust, leave him to work alone. Sweat rolled into his eyes and the corners of his mouth, soaked his chest. Sawdust coated his wet skin, and the whine of the single piston made his forehead throb. He worked as fast and hard as he could, and when Howard had trouble getting a long slab off the pile, went to help him instead of waiting with the saw running free in his hands.

He stepped over the low sawhorse to help his brother pull the railing free, and in stepping back, brought his foot against the blade. The engine changed pitch, there was a popping sound as the leather of his shoe snapped open, and suddenly he was sitting on the ground—he'd jumped, his mother said later, literally jumped—pulling off his shoe. His skin was not touched, but it was enough. The children closed in to look at his torn shoe and sock, his mother called questions from the porch—he remembered Nadine ran inside because she was afraid to look—and he imagined he heard the old men, mumbling, cackling, behind their screened windows.

*Do you remember how I jumped Howard? Ask Nadine if she remembers. I jumped and I've never really lit down since have I?*

"You're goddam lucky," Howard said after he turned off the saw. "You could just as damn well be bleeding to death right now. Why the hell don't you watch what you're doing, Harry?" He imagined himself hopping around the yard, spouting blood, transcribing raggy, scarlet figure eights on the grass, lying in a hospital bed with leg raised, foot swollen and truncated in bandages, clumping through life wearing an orthopedic shoe.

"That's it," he said to his brother. "I've had it for today. I've got to get a damn drink. Come on, Howie, I'll buy you a drink. I'm through for today." For any day. Their mother watched them without speaking as they left in Howard's car, her expression still quizzical. Could she have known he was deserting the job? *Do you remember her face, how she looked there, standing, Howard? I remember. I remember the Elbow Room too. They had a sign advertising their television set.*

It wasn't as if Harrison didn't do any work the next month. He painted the floor of the porch, yes, a dark forest green to match the trim, and he caulked and red-leaded the metal roof against rain. But he slept late in the mornings, waited for the mailman to bring job referrals, and in time was required to tell his mother no more lies; she ceased asking. *I ask you Howard how could I blame you? Nor do I blame you for selling and moving.*

Moved, because a Negro family moved in a block and a half away, and Nadine was afraid the streets wouldn't be safe nights.

Harrison got up and looked for a clock in the motel room, but there was none. He looked out the window across the court. The bar was still open, the music, but if the woman was still there, she was silent. He looked back at the unfinished, formless letter to Howard on the desk. He hadn't gotten to what he wanted to say to his brother, to Nadine, to All. *I only blame you for the porch. If we'd finished the porch who knows what I might have made of myself.*

Before he left to go to the bar, he checked to see that he had the key to his room and that everything was ready for the morning, his interview. A glance at the bathroom mirror reassured him; a stable, confident type; capable.

In the morning he'd clear his head with a shower and shave, breakfast lightly at the motel, and if they sold them at the registration desk—they always sold them—he'd dash off a card to Howard and Nadine to ask them if the people who bought the house complained about the unfinished porch. And to let them know where he was going to be, for the next few months anyway.

# I WOULDN'T I?

THE COMPOUND LEADER took the reports from the prisoner squad and platoon leaders like Lou; they wore special white canvas armbands that said *Squad Leader* or *Platoon Leader* under the big black *S* that all the prisoners wore. Then the compound leader read some announcements from his clipboard, checking them off one by one with a mechanical pencil. He had Lou fall out the last thing before he read off fatigue detail assignments. "Hey you, big Baxter," he said, and looked up from the clipboard to find Lou's face.

"Here sergeant," Lou said.

"Okay old Baxter, you fall yourself out to the billets and get in class A uniform. You're going to trial today. They'll be an escort from your company come to pick you up." In Lou's squad, where none of the MP personnel standing near the compound leader could hear them, some men made a few cracks.

"Say hello to my brother in Leavenworth for me, big old Baxter."

"I got money says Baxter don't get more than five years nor less than one. Cover me."

"Baxter don't want no court-martials, he's got it too good in jail."

"And I want to thank you kindly too," Lou called out back to the compound leader, then double-timed it back to his barracks. He meant it too. Over in Funston and Forsythe the barracks were all the T-types put up during the second world war, flimsy, hot in summer, and cold in winter, but the Fort Riley stockade was on the main post, the old part that went back to the cavalry days, so the prisoners' barracks and the admin buildings inside the fence were all old horse barns, built of stone with thick walls that kept the heat out no matter how bad it got out in the open compound under that August sun. It was a perfect cool, moist sleeping temperature inside all the time.

He changed from fatigues to suntans, but didn't bother to change his boots for brogans. He didn't know if he was supposed to wear his armband on his suntans or not, so folded it and put it in his hip pocket just in case. He stretched out on his bunk for a snooze; he was tired. The thing was he felt just mostly always tired these days. And the stockade was about as comfortable a place as any to rest up if only they'd let a man alone and didn't send him out on fatigue details six days every week.

Old big Baxter liked it in jail, someone said. Didn't he? He liked it in this jail all right, so long as he had to be in some jail at all. The town clink in Whipple, Tennessee, now that place purely smelled. They had one big drunk tank there, and if the turnkey emptied the slop bucket during a weekend it was an accident. He didn't miss Whipple, Tennessee, not one bit, because every time he thought Whipple he thought the smell of that drunk tank's slop bucket.

Compared to the detention and disciplinary compound at Eta Jima, Japan, this stockade was a regular hotel. Eta Jima was just tent flys inside a barbed wire fence, but it rained every day the week Lou was there under investigation for murdering a Japanese, and besides, his mouth had been full of stitches then. He was dreaming and fingering the scars around his mouth one minute, and then he must have dozed off, because the gate runner was shaking him awake the next.

"Big man Baxter," the runner said, "there's a skinny, no-assed man out by the sallyport with a gun to take you away."

"Ain't there?" Lou said.

"There is. Court-martialed today, the man said, huh Lou? They gonna give you the time today, right? How much time you figure you're subject to get, old big Baxter?"

"I'll inform you straight," Lou said. "Three months I'll pull. I can do three months standing on my head under water. Six months I'm not about to pull."

"Would you ex-scape, Louie?"

"Wouldn't I?" He walked across the compound to the sallyport with the runner following him like his pet hound. He was let through the first gate. Inside he looked around for his escort to see if it was maybe one of his friends from the motor pool, but the escort must have been standing back in the shadows of the guardshack. "Good morning to you, Corporal Pollard," he said to the MP who came over to shake him down. Lou took off his garrison cap and showed him it was empty inside, nothing stuck away in the lining.

"Frisking you is like frisking a small mountain, Baxter," Pollard said. "I never knew you were a Pfc."

"You must not of been here when I came in. I had it sewed on all my suntans and my OD's, but I never put it on my fatigues. I won't be one long no way." Pollard patted his armpits, crotch, and the bottoms of his trousers where they bloused over his boot tops.

"Well good luck to you anyhow, Baxter. Say, would you mind telling me where you got all those marks on your lips if it's not too personal? I always wanted to ask you that."

"I was in a hatchet battle," Lou said, "and everybody had a hatchet but me." When Pollard was opening the padlock on the outer sallyport gate, Lou saw his escort come out of the guardshack shadows. He didn't recognize him. He was a kid maybe five and a half feet tall, eighteen or nineteen, a private, his suntan uniform not fitting any too well. He wore a scuffed helmet liner that looked too big, and he wore army issue eyeglasses, plain steel frames and bows. His pistol belt was so loose the holster hung too far down on his leg, like some bony little four-eyed cowboy.

Lou was about to say hello to the escort when the Sergeant of the Guard came up behind the kid and yanked the .45 out of the open holster. "Damnit, soldier," the Sergeant of the Guard said, "when you push a prisoner, always push him loaded." He spun the kid around and grabbed the clip out of his hand. He jammed it into the handle and cocked the action to feed a round into the chamber. "There now," said the Sergeant of the Guard. "Now you can push him anywheres you need to go," and he dropped the .45 back into its holster.

Now Lou was close enough to read his nametag. *Yingst* the nametag said—now what kind of a name was a *Yingst?* The sergeant went back into the guardshack. "I do hope we're not going to hoof it all the way to Funston, Yingst," he said. "It's one hot day."

"The jeep's up the hill," Yingst said, but didn't move, so Lou started up the stone steps to the main post street, and the kid just naturally fell in behind about a dozen paces back. Then the compound gate runner took it into his head to cup his hands at his mouth and yell out a wisecrack.

"Boot him one square in his little fanny, Louie! Take that gun away from him an' make him ask you polite for it back, you big Baxter!" Neither Lou nor the kid Yingst said anything.

The jeep driver was C. T. Sneed, a good friend. He winked at Lou, and Lou flipped C. T. Sneed a mock salute. He waited for Yingst to catch up. "After you, son," he said.

"Are you trying to be funny or something?" Yingst said. He had one wild, cocked eye, and every couple of seconds he squinted and worked his forehead like his GI glasses didn't help him to see so very good. "The prisoner rides up front next to the driver and the guard gets in back. I know that well enough." Lou looked at C. T. Sneed, who grinned and shrugged like he didn't know this Yingst kid either.

"I certainly got no objections to riding next to old C. T. Sneed, and that's fact," Lou said, and climbed in, but Yingst didn't smile. The metal was scorching hot where Lou touched the jeep.

"Just don't think you're funny," Private Yingst said, and got into the jump seat, climbing over the mounted spare tire. C. T. Sneed started the engine. Lou turned around to speak to the kid and jumped himself when the kid half jumped out of the seat. "Don't get funny," he said again.

"That boy in there that hollered that to us," Lou said, watching this Yingst closely, "he's just a big-mouthed boy likes to yell at people. That's why he's on the inside. I was just wanting to say he's just a boy talks a lot," Lou said, because he'd seen from the first Yingst was afraid of him, and he didn't like that feeling behind him.

"I didn't worry about it if that's what you think," Yingst said, and Lou liked that even less, because it was a pure lie.

"You think maybe old Louie Baxter'd like some good company chow before he goes to see the man for trial?" C. T. Sneed said.

"Wouldn't he?" Lou said, and made himself forget the kid in the jump seat. Sneed put the jeep in gear and drove them to the company area in Camp Funston.

They got to the big consolidated headquarters mess right in the middle of the meal. The word was out that he was coming, all his friends from the motor pool waiting for him. "I saved you the seat of honor, Louie, that is if our friend here don't have objection." Lou looked back at Yingst.

"Just go on," he said. "I know he's supposed to eat lunch first."

Lou went in and his friends hollered out to him. Tired as he felt, he gave them a big smile and shook hands all around the table where they'd saved a seat for him, but to tell the truth he'd a lot rather been still snoozing back on his cot in the stockade. "Aren't you eating?" he asked Yingst when the kid didn't take a tray off the rack and fall in behind him in the chow line.

"I can't very well sit down and eat and be your guard at the same time, can I?" Lou set his tray on the steam table and stepped over to talk to him. "You stay right where you are," Yingst said.

"I just want to talk private with you."

"Talk from there. I hear you. Don't come so close to me. I'm your guard, remember?" and the Yingst kid smiled.

"Well you don't have to take it so serious, son. I'm not subject to run off on you—"

"Not while I'm guarding you you're not, that's for sure."

"—well. Just relax, son. I'm only interested in getting some of these good vittles." The menu was Swiss steaks that day. The cook serving on the line forked Lou out a big one and dropped it on his tray with a wink.

"You're looking awfully good in your war suit today, Mr. Baxter," the mess sergeant said to him.

"Probably it's the last day I'll wear it for a while," Lou said. Yingst followed him right to his table and leaned back against the windowsill while he ate. When he was finished his motor pool friends all shook hands with him and wished him luck at the court-martial. Even the first sergeant stopped by at his table when he came in for coffee and wished him good luck, too. "I'm ready to go if you are, son," Lou said.

"Don't call me son. I don't like it."

"Any way you say," and they went off to the JAG building for the trial, the kid Yingst ten or a dozen paces back. The afternoon sun turned on like an oven, and there wasn't a stir in the air except for one little dust-devil that scootered down the shoulder of the road toward Lou and on past him to Yingst. Lou looked back over his shoulder and laughed, but Yingst didn't join in; he just walked along with the heel of his hand resting on the butt of the .45 like some kid playing at cowboy. "You know you don't *have* to not talk to me," Lou said. "I just *might* appreciate some talk."

"I didn't hear anyone talking to me before now," this Yingst said. Still he didn't change the expression on his face, but later, outside the courtroom while the court-martial board was getting seated, he did talk a little.

"You were in Korea, weren't you?" Yingst said.

"Wasn't I? You know that, friend."

"I know that from that patch you have on your right shoulder. That's the 45th Division. The thunderbird."

"That's the one. General P. D. Ginder commanding. Was you there too?"

"You must think you're being funny again. I've only been in the army seven months."

"I figured you were new in the company. I never seen you around before today."

"I've been in the company five months almost. I was in basic training in the 87th and then they shipped me to headquarters because I had typing in high school."

"I never seen you I guess," Lou said.

"I've been here, but I don't have a regular job, like in the motor pool or supply. I take care of the dayroom and sometimes I help the mail clerk, or the first sergeant gives me a special job to do like this one guarding you. First I was in the motor pool, but McLennon kicked me out for smashing a three-quarter when I was learning to drive. I never learned to drive. He never gave me a fair chance. He just kicked me out, so now I fiddle around the dayroom all day."

"I don't get to the dayroom much, I'll admit. Old McLennon's a good enough motor sergeant. I think he was in the 5th RCT in Korea, same as old Sneed, same as the CO, too. McLennon's a good old boy but I grant you he's tempered sometimes."

"I've seen you around the company though, you and those guys like Sneed at chow from the motor pool, your friends. You're the one who socked Lieutenant Loeffler, aren't you?"

"Ain't I? You know I am. I didn't hit him though, I just threatened to, which is just as good for court-martialing as if I did. You know old Loeffler too, do you? I don't mind him so much, really. He's not but a snot ROTC motor officer, but he's okay I guess."

"You're one of the first guys in the company I've talked to in five months," Yingst said. "I don't know anybody in this company." Lou unfolded his arms and looked at the kid and was about to say something, but his defense counsel, a colored first lieutenant from quartermaster, came out of the courtroom and told the escort to bring his prisoner in.

It was a quick trial. Lieutenant Loeffler was the only witness called. He told the straight truth, word for word, of what took place. He was good enough to say that he thought Pfc Baxter would never have threatened him if he hadn't been intoxicated at the time, and also that Pfc Baxter was a very efficient vehicle driver, an asset to the motor pool. The colored lieutenant didn't call any character witnesses, but he did read a list of Lou's decorations from Korea, forgetting that he got two Purple Hearts and not just one. This was a mistake. It caused the prosecution officer to mention Lou's general court-martial for murder while a member of the Eighth Army in Japan.

"He oughtn't to mention that, sir, I was found not guilty on that," he whispered to his defense counsel.

"We'd better not make a fuss," the Negro said. He was very nervous at his first court-martial. Also the prosecution read off Lou's page in the company punishment book: two restrictions, one with extra duty, for being disorderly in the barracks at night. Lou, his counsel, and his escort went outside in the hall again while the board deliberated his guilt. The lieutenant excused himself and went across the street to the Service Club to get a Coca-Cola.

"What was that about murdering?" Yingst asked him as soon as the officer was gone.

"That's a long story."

"I have time."

"The army thought I killed a Jap, but it was a friend of mine did it. Both of us was not guilty on that."

"Was it really the other guy who did it?"

"Damn straight it was! What'd you ask for if you won't believe me? I got other things to worry about right now. Let me alone." By rights he should have been worried about what the board was doing, but nothing seemed so important except that tired feeling running all through him. Hot as it was, he'd as soon gone to sleep right there with that ugly Yingst kid watching him.

"How'd you get those scars on your mouth?"

"Will you let me alone?" Actually, it *was* his buddy old

Forbes who killed the Jap. Lou told him to. The Jap was some uncle or something, kin to the little cho-san he and Forbes came to see that night. Small as he was, he *could* fight. Forbes was fumbling around in the bedroom of the house there at Eta Jima looking for something to club the Jap with. Lou wrestled him to the floor, but the Jap rolled on top of him and all of a sudden, like some damn animal, bit right into Lou's mouth with his teeth. With the little Jap there holding on, with his teeth meeting right through Lou's lips, Forbes came over with the gun at last. He whacked the Jap alongside his head, but he didn't loosen his teeth. "Shoot him!" Lou yelled as best he could like that. Forbes put the muzzle into the Jap's ear and shot him. Together they pried his jaws loose.

"What's wrong, are you ashamed of where you got the scars?" Yingst said.

"Would you believe me if I told you a man's teeth did it?"

"No."

"All right then."

"Say for a minute you really didn't do the murder and your friend did. If you were in his place, would you have done it?"

"Wouldn't I?" Lou said. The lieutenant came back and said he thought they had a good chance. The court's law officer called them back in. Lou was found guilty of all charges and specifications, sentenced to reduction in grade from private first class to private, forfeiture of two-thirds of all pay and allowances for a period of six months, and six months' confinement to the post stockade.

"We'll appeal it. There's an automatic review of sentence by the next higher command," the lieutenant assured him. "Don't take it so hard, Baxter."

"The whole thing makes me tired, sir," Lou said. Yingst

was given a carbon copy of the court's findings and told to escort the prisoner to his company to await the decision of the reviewing authority. They didn't speak on the walk to the company. At the orderly room the first sergeant told them to go over to Lou's old barracks and relax until the review was phoned in.

"They just might cut the stockade time off, Baxter," the first sergeant said. But that was only like wishing him good luck. The best, the very best Lou could hope for was maybe a reduction of the sentence to three months, and this seemed like too much effort.

It was clean-linen day in the barracks. The bunk springs were bare, the striped mattress ticks rolled up at the head of each cot. The T-type barracks were hotter inside than out; Lou took off his necktie and opened his khaki shirt.

"You get on that side," Yingst said, pointing. "I'll stay on this side so I can watch you."

"I'll tell you something, young man," Lou said. "This morning I swore I'd run off if they gave me six months . . ."

"Is that right?"

"Yes it's right. But just now I couldn't care less if it was six years at Leavenworth. I'm laying down to rest on old Sneed's bunk here and I'll thank you to let me be."

"Go ahead," Yingst said, and it couldn't have been more than a minute and Lou was asleep. He didn't remember anything but the ending of a dream about a widow woman in Whipple, Tennessee, he'd loved for a while once. His eyes just opened up when he woke, and there was this Yingst kid propped up on a bunk across the aisle with his legs crossed, his face all screwed up, taking a bead on him with the .45.

"What the hell are you doing?" Lou said. He didn't move his hands from behind his head. He'd sweated through his shirt, and his neck felt wet.

"He's awake," the kid said, and lowered the pistol to his side. It clanked against the metal springs.

"I hope you remember the man jacked one into the chamber there at the stockade." He eased his hands out and laid them open in his lap.

"I have to practice, don't I? I never fired familiarization on the .45. Just the M-1 and carbine. I'd have to know how to aim it if you got up and started running, wouldn't I?"

Lou kept his hands in sight. He listened for sounds in the company street, but it seemed empty. Wouldn't old C. T. Sneed be dropping in to talk if he could? Wouldn't they keep Sneed on standby to take Lou back to the stockade when the review came down? He wondered how long he'd been asleep.

"You know why the army developed the .45?" Yingst asked. He had the pistol in front of him again, but not pointed at Lou.

"No word on the review yet?" Lou said.

"Because they couldn't stop the rebels in the Philippines with a .38. They'd keep coming no matter how many times they were shot with a .38. These were the fanatics that fought us in the Spanish-American War. They developed the .45 and it stopped them. I used to read about guns all the time when I was in high school."

"Can I get up and get a drink of water?" Lou asked.

"I prefer you stay right there." Yingst pointed the pistol at him again.

"All right. All right whatever you say."

"Even somebody as big as you are, you couldn't take a .45 and still stand up. I've seen them fired on the range. The kick throws your arm up over your head. If you were coming at me and I shot you with a .45 right where you are now, you'd be knocked against the wall."

"Well I'm not about to be coming at you, see?"

"Did you ever kill anyone, Baxter?"

"I told you my friend killed that Jap, not me."

"No, I believe you about that. In Korea I mean. Any North Koreans."

"I don't know. I shot at some but I don't know certain I killed them."

"I could shoot you right now, Baxter. I could just shoot you and say you were coming for me. No one could say different. I heard if a guard kills a prisoner they promote him one stripe and take and transfer him then. Is that the truth?"

"Why would you want to kill me? I never even knew you before this."

"I could do it. Nobody could prove you weren't getting away."

"Now why should you do that?" Lou said. He listened to the company street, but there wasn't anyone out there. He was probably near twice as old as this Yingst, and very tired of being in jails and in the army; he was tired of men picking fistfights with him just because he was the biggest man in sight. He wanted a drink of water. Yingst kept the pistol on him, squinting his eyes behind those GI glasses. He thought of Forbes and C. T. Sneed and of a widow woman he'd loved once for a while in Whipple, Tennessee. He thought of the smell of that drunk tank in the Whipple town clink, and he was tired and scared.

He raised up a little on the bunk. This Yingst kid wouldn't shoot him. "You wouldn't just here and now shoot me, would you?" Lou said.

"Wouldn't I?" Yingst said.

# WAITING

ROY MEANT to leave a note for his daughter, but he forgot that too. He was dressed, sitting on the couch in the living room instead of in his own special tilting chair, just to make sure he wouldn't drop off and miss the taxi when it came for him. He had the volume on his hearing aid turned all the way up to be certain he'd catch the doorbell ringing. He went so far as to fumble for the inside pocket of his suitcoat to get his pen, but then he dropped a cigarette ash on the carpet and was busy rubbing it into the nap with his shoe, because Dottie worried so much about his smoking, even though she tried not to show it.

He got a little dizzy bending over to fluff up the carpet nap with his fingers, and when his head cleared his cigarette was burning close to his fingers. By the time he'd pressed it out carefully in the large ashtray on the coffee table, he'd forgotten all about a note to let Dottie know where he was going. After that he concentrated on waiting for the cab-driver to ring the doorbell, going over the contents of the three suitcases in his mind to see that he had everything he'd need at home. Just waiting was tiring, and enough to make him forget everything else for the moment.

Roy had nothing to do in his daughter's house but wait. Since he'd lived at Dottie's he'd been unable to sleep well, but still he waited for the day to end with the eleven o'clock news on television. Dottie got up to take the after-dinner coffee cups and saucers into the kitchen; Clark, his son-in-law, stood up and stretched and tucked his shirt neatly into his belt, though it would be off and in the hamper in a few minutes. Roy slipped off the headphones Clark had rigged to the TV for him so he could hear without turning the set all the way up. By eleven his granddaughters were already in bed and asleep. Clark always helped him up out of the tilting chair where he sat to relieve the chronic swelling in his ankles. "Time to hit it, huh, Roy?" Clark usually said.

"I'll leave the lights on in the bathroom for you when I get through, Papa," Dottie said. They stepped close to speak to him, as if he read lips too, and he held out the hearing aid in his shirt pocket for them. He could see by the deliberate way their mouths moved that they spoke very loud. Dottie kissed him goodnight.

"Sleep well, darling," Roy said. By the time he'd undressed, hanging and folding everything, they were in their bedroom, and he could shuffle to the bathroom in his slippers and robe. He read while he waited for sleep, and at the right moment laid his magazine aside and snapped off the bedlight over his head.

He slept an hour, sometimes as long as two, and then he woke with no memory of having dreamed, and his mind was perfectly clear, his vision sharp, the moment he found his glasses. He left his light off and stayed in bed as long as he could, then put his hearing aid on and went to the kitchen because he could sleep again only if he ate something. He walked slowly, steadying himself on the arms of chairs, the edge of the dining room table. He depressed the toaster knob gradually, released it before the cycle was over and it popped. He heated water for his Sanka, ate, and felt triumphant if his daughter didn't wake before he was back in his bed again.

This happened at least twice each night. If it was past five he stayed, smoking and drinking Sanka, waiting in the rising grey light of the kitchen for Dottie's radio alarm to go on. They had breakfast together.

They ate, and he waited for them to leave; one of his contributions was to clear and wash the breakfast dishes so Dottie could have time for an extra cup of coffee. Alone, he sat with more Sanka and his cigarettes at the kitchen table, waiting for his digestion to settle and strength to gather in his legs to carry him to the sink. He read the morning newspaper and waited for the mailman to bring his magazine subscriptions. A rare day brought a personal letter to answer, a form to fill out. He waited for noon to eat lunch. He waited for the mantel clock to strike Westminster chimes, waited for the repetition of news in the evening paper, waited for Dottie and Clark and the girls to return. They always had a little cocktail hour at six-thirty; his son-in-law always said that nobody made a whiskey sour like Roy's.

And he began to forget things. In the night, passing Dottie's bedroom from the kitchen after his toast and Sanka, he paused, and must have started talking out loud to himself; he couldn't remember the thought that arrested him there. "Papa?" Dottie said from her bed. Roy turned the volume up on his hearing aid as she turned on the light. "Papa, are you up? What are you doing, Papa?" He looked down and saw that his hands were shaking, felt the cold night draft along the floor sink deep in his ankles. "Are you all right, Papa?"

"I'm fine. I'm going to bed," Roy said, but it was a fight to keep from falling on the way back to his bed, where he had to rub his feet and ankles several minutes to get the circulation back. Little moments disappeared like that.

Just after they left one morning, he lit a cigarette and

moved the steaming cup of Sanka closer to him on the kitchen table. One moment it was too hot to drink, and his cigarette lay freshly burning on the lip of his ashtray. Then, the next, the next he knew, he looked and the Sanka was almost cold and the cigarette was a white thread of ash right up to its filter, and he couldn't be certain how much time was gone on the kitchen clock. He watched himself all that day, but said nothing about it to Dottie.

He sat down one morning to write to Bill Neil, pecking out the letter on the portable at the desk in the dining room with two fingers. *Hello Bill,* he wrote. *I have some sad news for you this time. My darling Eva is gone from me forever Bill. She is not just sick but gone now for good. The doctors say she has an embolism which means she does not know me or Dottie when we go to the nursing home to see her. Yes she has to be in a nursing home for good now Bill. It is only a question of time before she will die of it. It is no good to be my age Bill. Eva lived to be seventy-six years old.*

He caught himself there, forcing a laugh because Eva had been dead four months, he'd lived with Dottie for nearly five, and Bill Neil made it up from Quincy for the funeral. Seventy-five himself, he led his totally blind wife, who Roy thought he heard crying behind him while the Methodist minister gave a short eulogy in front of Eva's casket. He remembered the minister saying she had more than her three score and ten years, and we should be grateful to God for this. Before the eulogy, the organ played and Dottie introduced her friends to Bill, saying, "This is Papa's friend, Bill Neil. He and Papa met in Nashville in 1910," and the friends all said, fifty years, more than fifty years, my goodness isn't that wonderful!

Roy tore the letter to Bill Neil in small pieces and stuffed them in the bottom of the wastebasket in the dining room.

He'd stopped laughing about it by the time he put the typewriter away, and it wasn't really laughing; it was what he had to do to keep himself from crying.

He napped in the chair with his feet up, woke, and forgetting, tried to get up as quickly and smoothly as a man Clark's age. Halfway up he felt his balance go, so poised, flapping his arms like an injured or arthritic bird about to plummet out of the sky, until he stood firm or collapsed heavily back into the soft chair, or one of the girls came running to take his arm.

He sat smoking, with a magazine or watching television, and was shocked to notice the yellowing thin back of his own hand, liver spotted, the blue veins standing out in relief. Shaving, he was suddenly surprised to see the triangle of glossy white hair that remained on his head, the dewlap and wattles he needed to pull taut for his razor, as queer to his touch as a stranger's skin.

He tried to tick off the days with schedules of little tasks, but even forgot to wash up the breakfast dishes once or twice a week, and once, just before the others came back, found a grocery list he'd drawn up and left on top the television; he hadn't gone shopping since he lived alone in his own house on Pacific Street, the first few weeks Eva was in the nursing home where they diagnosed her embolism, when Clark came over on Saturdays in the station wagon to take him to the supermarket. There was no time to burn the list, so he hid it in an old shoe, and never remembered it until the day he packed up his things to go back home.

Yet some things were clear. He and Clark watched a prize fight on television, drinking beer from the cans. "He's taking a hell of a whipping," Clark said.

"How's that?" Roy took off the headphones and inserted the hearing aid earpiece.

"I say he's whaling hell out of him."

"You should have seen Willard," Roy said. And he remembered it all. The outdoor ring in Ohio, Willard as big as a tower, contemptibly fat and soft, Dempsey as hard and tan as an Indian, the sunshine, everyone wearing white shirts and summer straws. 1919: Roy had been married less than four years, had a contract to telegraph a report of the fight to New Orleans for the *Times-Picayune*. "I saw him on the El station platform in Chicago just after the fight, too," Roy said.

"Who's that?"

"Willard. I was talking about Jess Willard. He looked like a big fat farm boy that'd been through a grinder. They used to say Dempsey had plaster casts on his fists." He stopped talking because they wanted to see this fight on TV, and because Clark wasn't really interested, and because it was enough for him to remember it all, and see the sun-bleached ring apron, Dempsey's back muscles working as he flailed away, Willard the fat farm boy like a tattered giant on the El platform in Chicago. It was better.

The conversation at dinner passed outside and beyond Roy until someone mentioned San Francisco. "I was in San Francisco three years after the quake," he said.

"What, Papa?" Dottie said. His granddaughters politely stopped talking to listen to him.

"I just said I was in San Francisco once," he said, and went back to his dinner, not bothering to turn up his hearing aid, knowing Dottie looked at her husband for a moment, that Clark glared at the girls to make them stop staring at their grandfather; Roy didn't care. He thought: San Francisco. He thought of Spider Kelly's saloon on the Barbary Coast, the mirror behind the bar decorated with imitation spiderwebs, the trapdoor in the floor they said Kelly himself used to throw when a ship needed deckhands, a water tumbler of whiskey selling for thirty cents, and this was enough.

He pored over the box of photographs he'd brought with him when he moved in. "Here's one of you and me when you weren't very old," he said to his granddaughter.

"Granpa, that's mother, isn't it?" she said. Roy looked again, said nothing. It was him, nearly forty years ago, with Dottie not more than four or five, holding his hand on the beach at Lake Michigan. "We both look like mother when she was little," his granddaughter said of herself and her sister, but Roy had taken his earpiece out.

He found what he thought was a gold coin one day, looking through a drawer, thinking it must be a souvenir of some kind, until he looked close, saw it was a silver dollar wrapped in gold foil, remembered it came off the little money tree, a centerpiece at the party he and Eva were given on their fiftieth anniversary.

He found the key there, too. He found it in one of the top dresser drawers in the curtained alcove that was his bedroom in his daughter's house. He was looking for something, a handkerchief, cigarettes, he forgot just what, and the heavy brass key lying hidden at the back of the narrow drawer stabbed his groping fingers.

He held it up to the light from the alcove's only window, where Dottie had kept an ivy plant before he moved in. He turned it over in the light, wondering where, when? Then he remembered, the key, the lock it would fit, the door, his own house on Pacific Street. He decided then, and checked the time on the railroad watch he wore on the end of a chain; it was too late today. In an hour they would be home from work and school.

He put the key in one hand and closed his fingers tightly over it. The impression of its outline and its sharp-edged grooves in his palm would not let him forget. The key grew warm and moist in his fist, and he found it difficult to force his fingers open. He stuck it next to the watch in his vest pocket and went out through the curtain to the living room to wait for the others to get back; they'd have a cocktail and talk about what happened that day in school and at work.

The cabdriver had to ring four times before Roy heard him and went to let him in. "I'll have to ask you to give me a hand with the bags. I can't handle that kind of thing anymore," Roy said to the squat little man wearing a black visored cap without a badge, a pencil behind his ear. He left Dottie's house without looking back.

"Hang on here and I'll help you negotiate the steps," the driver said.

"I'm okay."

"No, just hang on while I get the bags in the cab," and he waited for him because his legs felt weak. It was too warm a day for the suit he wore, and the sun made him squint painfully.

They passed a cemetery on the way to Pacific Street. "Is that Roselawn?" Roy said. The cabbie said he thought so. "My wife's buried there. In the Masonic section. I'm a Mason thirty-seven years. I was married fifty-two years some months. You can't see it from here, I guess." Either the driver didn't hear, or he had no answer. He set the bags on the front porch of the house for Roy, then walked him up to the door. "You sure you're okay?"

"Just my legs. My goddamn legs give out when I sit the same way too long," Roy said, and the man looked back at him like he'd never heard swearing before.

"You're all set here?"

"I've got a doorkey, haven't I? Do I look like a housebreaker?" He paid him and tipped him a dollar. "Listen here. I need to lay in some groceries. How'd you like to come back here tomorrow morning and take me shopping?"

"I can do that if you want," he said. "A fella your age, you say you're okay here? It looks empty here."

"I live here," Roy said. He opened the door with the key to show him, and the driver set the bags inside the door for him before he left, pushing his cap onto the back of his head to wipe his brow as he thanked Roy for the tip. Roy never got the bags unpacked, never moved them in from the front hall of the Pacific Street house, because he went in to rest up first, and he was still sitting in the same chair when Dottie and Clark came for him.

He sat down to rest, and maybe he slept, he wasn't sure. There was very little left in the house now. In the bookcase were Eva's cookbooks and the graded Spanish readers she'd accumulated when she tried to learn the language, and rows of his old *National Geographics* and *Reader's Digests*. There was a great gaping emptiness where the tilting chair had been before Clark hauled it over to their house. The cabinet was still there, and the dinner table, but there had been over a dozen bird figurines on the cabinet, Eva's collection, and the shelves behind glass were bare vaults, and no place mats or candlesticks on the table.

The air was musty, the house closed so long, so perhaps he slept, dreamed, or perhaps he was losing his grasp of time, of the present, as Eva had before she died. Once he thought he heard a whistle from the kitchen, the way Eva had whistled to get his attention when she was busy at the gas range and he read with his hearing aid off.

It all happened very quickly. He heard the whistle, or in his mind there remained the impression, the sense of having heard it, so many times, and he called out, "Eva?" He waited a moment, said again, "Eva," then sat back in the chair content with the echo of an echo of a whistle, listening so intently as it faded that he never heard the door open when Dottie and Clark, the girls waiting outside in the station wagon, came in to take him back home. The cabdriver had stopped by and told them where Roy was only a little before Dottie was ready to call the police.

"You could have called me here," Roy said.

"You know the phone was disconnected, Papa," she said. "If you knew how I felt when we came home and you weren't there . . ." She was angry, he saw, and still a little scared, and she held his face in both hands and kissed him twice.

"Come on now, Roy," her husband said. "It's so hot in here you're all sweated up."

"Why did you do it, Papa? You know you can't go out alone, Papa. You know you can't live here anymore. Are you all right? Are you crying, Papa?" she said.

"What?" He heard, but she didn't repeat it, and finally he was not crying, and he could smile and say hello to his granddaughters when he reached the station wagon at the curb, Clark behind them with the bags. He said he was all right. He borrowed Clark's handkerchief to dry his face; he seemed to have forgotten to put one in his pocket when he dressed to leave. When they were home they had whiskey sours for their little cocktail hour, as if nothing had happened.

Clark had to go out after dinner, and the girls were in their bedrooms. Roy sat in his special chair with a magazine, pretending to read, and really reading, too, but pretending. His hearing aid was off, but he knew whenever his daughter stepped in from the kitchen to check on him, still uncertain, or seeing that he hadn't dozed off with a cigarette that would burn the house down.

In the corner of his eye he saw the light and shadow change as she came in, stood to watch, left again to finish her dishes. He sat in the chair with his feet up to relieve the swelling in his ankles, reading the words on the page, pretending to read, while he waited.

# HASKELL HOOKED ON THE NORTHERN CHEYENNE

March 3d

Fr. Cyprian Hogan, OFM
Cheyenne Mission School
Broadaxe, Montana

Dear Fr. Cyprian:

Enclosed please find my check for five dollars ($5.00) in response to your appeal.

My wife and I appreciate the gift of the little plastic teepee, and send our best wishes to you in your work among the northern Cheyenne. We're both sure the money will be put to good use, and only regret it is not more.

Yours Very Truly,
H. Haskell

March 19th

Fr. Cyprian Hogan, OFM
Cheyenne Mission School
Broadaxe, Montana

Dear Fr. Cyprian:

Enclosed find my check for $5.00 in response to your second appeal in as many weeks.

From the letter of thanks you sent after the first check I feel you've gotten off on an unfounded assumption. We're not fellow Catholics. It was the "Dear Friend in Christ" salutation in your letter—or does that just mean someone who appears to feel the same way about things like charity without belonging to the same club?

My wife attended Bible camp for two summers while in junior high, so you could call us generic Protestants; anyway we're not Catholic. If we did attend a church regularly it would have to be one of the Lutheran varieties. Please don't misunderstand.

I like to call myself a liberal, and we both realize your mission helps the Cheyenne regardless of *their* religious affiliations—I remember your statement in the first appeal to the effect that only a small percentage of the tribe are practicing Catholics.

I only want the record straight. I give because I want to. Again, we send along our moral support. I know nothing about the problems you face, the daily lives of the Indians, but have some general ideas about poverty, bad nutrition, illiteracy, etc. prevailing on our federal reservations.

Yours Very Truly,

H. Haskell

P.S. You might like to know the little plastic teepee's in good hands. We have no children, but I gave it to a neighbor child, who was quite pleased. A miracle, her mother came over to thank me, and she's never done more before this than nod hello as she pulls out in her station wagon. I guess it's not the sort of toy one can buy in the stores here.

April 17th

Fr. Cyprian Hogan, OFM
Cheyenne Mission School
Broadaxe, Montana

Dear Fr. Cyprian:

What is it with you, Father? No, that's wrong. I don't want to offend, vent spleen, etc. But you're imposing, and I've got to express it. My wife warned me not to write—"Just simply ignore it," she said. "Is there a law that says you have to answer all the junk mail you get?" But you owe me a hearing.

In two weeks' time we received two appeals from you for donations to your work among the northern Cheyenne. I sent you $10.00. The canceled checks have already come back from my bank ("He didn't waste any time cashing in," my wife said when she was going over the monthly statement).

I hoped I conveyed good will, a recognition of your need, and I hoped—in vain I see now—you understood my position, that in good will you would not try to take advantage; now I get a third appeal for money. Let me be understood.

I am not wealthy. My salary is *exactly* $6,400 per annum (all right, so I get a little more each June when we work evenings on inventory). If you're interested (I doubt this), I make my living as a technical writer.

I write: technical manuals to accompany industrial air conditioning and heat transference units, explaining operation and maintenance for the layman; the text of advertising brochures used by our sales engineers; short articles on business conditions (marketing prospects, government regulations, technical developments, credit prospects for the near future) for a monthly trade magazine published by my employer.

Ye Gods, if I was rich wouldn't my checks have been larger? Wouldn't I beat the income tax with huge gifts, trust funds to see Indian orphans through graduate school? Wouldn't I sign over the deeds to properties to you, endow a chair in some university to study your problems? You abuse me.

Don't I give enough? My newsboy comes to the door in the evening to demand a contribution for summer camps for kids like himself—I give, not much, but give. College dropouts come around with magazine subscriptions to get trips to Europe. Brownies come in uniform to sell their cookies; I eat them for lunch faithfully. A neighbor (who holds loud parties we are never invited to) comes with a clipboard and informs me everyone is pledging twenty dollars for the ambulance service. I mail a buck to both political parties to keep democracy strong.

I'm not safe on the streets. Little Leaguers jump me on the way out of the bank with tin cans because they want an electric scoreboard. I get a Buddy Poppy each for wife and self. The Salvation Army surrounds me on the asphalt parking lot in the shopping center. At work, the United Fund sends me an IBM card via one of the girls in the steno pool. What is it with these people? I ask. "We've got to live here, don't we?" my wife says. I grin and give.

And now my name's on some religious sucker list. Because I've given you ten you think I'll give a hundred. I call halt. An unsolicited plastic teepee does not obligate me; I know the law. Catholics may be bound by oath or faith or mortal sin to support you. I am not.

How many of those printed formats do you have at the ready? Save it for someone else; I'm not a colored pin on a map, no target in your war to save the Red Man. I'm young, not thirty yet, owe on house and car, support a wife, heavily insured, need to hire a tree surgeon to save the one big elm on my property, suspect our furnace won't make another winter through. Give me a break.

Understand. "And then you go and write him another check," my wife says in disgust, and now pretends to be watching television too intently to hear me when I speak. "I don't want him to misunderstand is all," I say. So, $5 more, to convince you of good will, that I intend no hurt. Take it in the spirit it is given.

Sincerely,
H. Haskell

April 28th

Fr. Cyprian Hogan, OFM
Cheyenne Mission School
Broadaxe, Montana

Dear Fr. Cyprian:

I have received your long letter. You say: the force that carries you out there is the same spirit of charity you appeal to in me. Will it work to let you forgive me too?

What can I say? How kneel, sackcloth and ashes, beat the breast, how *mea culpa* from a thousand miles away via air mail? The whole thing reeks of ignorance and selfishness—all mine. Haskell thinks he understands, complains that your appeals are mass-produced, steals your time by demanding a personal reply.

I showed your letter to my wife. "I wish you'd just drop the whole thing," she said. "I should never have said those things. I didn't understand the way I do now," I said. No avail. "Just leave me out of it," she asks. Forgive her too.

When I started writing this she took the car and went over

to my brother's house to visit with his wife. Have you heard anything from my brother? I gave him your address and one of the pamphlets. "What am I supposed to do with this?" he said. "Send him something." At least he folded it and put it in his pocket. "You ever heard about charity at home?" he said. Then we took turns cutting his lawn with his new electric mower.

I plead ignorance in the first place. What did I know about the northern Cheyenne, Father? The story of Thomas, the little boy abandoned in the wrecked car by his parents because they couldn't feed him, that one did me in. Literally, real tears; fortunately I happened to be home alone then too. Sure I knew the Indians had it rough, but never the details. The TB, the drunkenness, infant mortality, what did I know? What I knew I only guessed. Thomas turning blue with the cold in that rusted junker, asking how far down in the milk bottle he could drink, here I was ignorant. Can you forgive?

The same for the history pamphlets. I had ideas, broken treaties, destroying the buffalo herds, but that's all from the movies. My brother read the one about Shivington's massacre of the women and children in the village. "They had that on TV a while back, I think," he said. "This is where it happened," I said, "here, these people I'm telling you about." "I know it happened," he said, "When the program started it said it was based on an actual fact." What does he know?

I tried getting angry, the Bureau of Indian Affairs, the Secretary of the Interior (I don't even know his name), the President, affluent citizens of Montana. No good. It all came out shame in the end.

Then comes selfishness. Watch out here for self-pity.

Sometimes there's nothing to hold on to. I mean, wife, work, responsibilities, installment payments, become a little too much. I get afraid I can't hold it together for long, pieces are going to fall out, and where are we all then? Tangled up, I can't see out: it makes me selfish.

A few minutes ago (my wife still isn't back—she must be staying for the late show. Out the picture window, the last visible porchlight blinked off—no parties tonight)—a few minutes ago I promised myself not to talk about my problems. But to apologize I need to be understood.

Believe it, I work hard. If I'm a success, industrial air conditioners are sold, stock dividends are voted (I don't own much yet), but where am I? I go to sleep at night promising to be ready to eat the world the next day, but it's hard to concentrate with the township's teenagers peeling the corner at the end of the block. I must dream. The resolve to be enthusiastic is sapped when the clock radio buzzes—"I suppose it won't do to heat up last night's coffee for you, it's got to be fresh-made," my wife says. How would you feel?

Do priests get up before the sun to pray? Is that me, the swollen face shaving in the bathroom mirror? The glazed eyes mine? My wife sings with the sizzling bacon in the breakfast nook, I stand dumb, looking at the sick elm in our yard. But I *do* get off to work. Do you understand me?

The days are longer now, still light when I come home, and I admit (why should I feel guilty?) to moments of peace after I greet my wife. We sit and watch the wars and speeches on film on the evening news, but who believes in that stuff? I drink a cold martini—okay, sometimes three—we talk about her day ("Did you see the moving van down towards the circle?" "Not when I came home, no. Who's moving out?" "I don't know their name, but there was a van there all day moving them out. It's the ones with the Imperial I told you about she's always driving by in." "So if you don't know their names who cares if they move?" "I didn't say I cared. I just told you.")

"Be a doll and mix one more," I say, "Two olives." All's well. I admit to moments of peace. Is it my fault they don't last?

I work in a cubicle in a large office (air conditioned). From my desk I can look out through glass panels at the busy secretaries in the steno pool, their ears plugged with dictaphones, eyes fixed on proof sheets. I never know their names until one comes around to collect donations for a wedding gift for Marie or Ardenne or Patty. I believe most of them are secret gum chewers. Engineers and marketing analysts and file clerks pass up and down aisles, say, "Here you go," when they toss a sheaf of paper into my *In* basket. Am I making sense?

I do try though. Excelsior. This Saturday I have decided to dig a small garden next to my garage. I was talking to the neighbor girl (she still has the teepee); she likes flowers, so I'll plant some along with a few vegetables. Back to the land.

Too tired to read it over, I hope what I've written is clear. The check, you'll see, is for ten this time, all I can do for now. Please continue to let me hear of your good work at the mission.

With sincere regard,
H. Haskell

May 29th

Fr. Cyprian Hogan, OFM
Cheyenne Mission School
Broadaxe, Montana

Dear Fr. Cyprian,

I thought I would not hear from you again. Good to know I am not forgotten. Is the little Indian chief doll authentic?

I mean, are headdress, decorations on the jacket, etc., the kind the Cheyenne wear—wore once? We've put him on the mantel-piece above the fireplace. My wife thinks he's cute. She calls him Sitting Bull, though I tell her he wasn't a Cheyenne. Or was he?

Not cute though. I've been analyzing the expression on his face. At first I said: Stoic. But that's all in the folded arms. Then: Courageous. But the brown painted eyes are too pale, no steel there. Sad? His back's too stiff. Finally I knew." He disapproves," I said to my wife. "Who what?" "He condemns." "What are you talking about, Haskell? Did I make that martootie too strong?" (She never uses my first name; nor do I—have you noticed? Hollis: my mother's maiden name—my brother got Jack, because he's the older.)

Unless I can learn to stare him (Sitting Bull) down I'm going to give him away too. "I tell you he doesn't like it," I said to my wife. "All that Indian wisdom in him disapproves." She said, "I think you're getting hooked on the northern Cheyenne, Haskell." Pure fantasy, Father, I assure you.

I wish this check could be more, but insurance all comes due at the same time: automobile, theft, fire, property, hospitalization, life.

Are there any extra pamphlets (describing the work) lying around in your office? I want to give some to friends and people at work.

Hoping to hear from you soon again,

H. Haskell

P.S. My garden progresses. Besides flowers, I planted sweet-corn, tomatoes, lettuce, beans—a landmark in this neighborhood. The little girl next door has never seen a tomato growing on a vine before in her life. "My daughter tells me you're planting regular vegetables and stuff here," her father said to me. He had come out in his slippers. "I'm Haskell," says I, hand extended. "I know who you are, I can read the writing on the mail box like anybody else, can't I? What do you want to do a thing like that for, can you tell me that?" "I like fresh corn." "You know this is gonna make my house look like hell too, don't you?" I promised to try and keep it small. "What did you expect him to say?" my wife said. Who could tell? What a world we live in, Father.

P.P.S. Next stop: public library—subject: American Indians.

June 16th

Dear Fr. Cyprian:

Pardon poor penmanship. I should be working, but who are we trying to kid? The wooden trays on my desk runneth over—copy piles up awaiting my initials (HHH—my mother's mother's maiden name was Hart). Through the glass wall around me I can see the steno I'm keeping idle. She is at a loss, buffs her nails, cleans her teeth with her tongue, changes typewriter ribbons, stacks carbons in readiness, switches off to the ladies room, returns too soon, panics, looks to me with terrified eyes, and I shake my head, pontifical as Sitting Bull on my mantel, and she slumps into her chair, defeated. The trouble is I get to thinking.

In the cafeteria a salesman said to me, "What's the use of working when the government takes a fifth of what I make before I even see it?" I swallowed my bread. "Do you know the Indians out in Montana make less a year, on the average, than you probably pay in taxes in a year?" He threw down his sandwich before he blasted me. "Oh for the Christ's sakes (he said it, Father, not me) Haskell, will you get off the goddamned boring damned Indians in Montana!" Dessert, two cupcakes under cellophane, passed in silence. What's the use?

I gave up reading the library books. "Are we doing anything tonight?" my wife asked. "Doing? I'm doing, I'm reading, right?" "If you're sticking your nose in a book all night, sure," and she turned on the television extra loud to get even. "Do you know all about Indians now?" the librarian asked when I returned them. What do I know?

Last Saturday I was weeding and cultivating my sweetcorn. Pleasant, hot sun, hands sore and back stiff, but my neighbor was watching me from his garage, pretending to putter with his son's go-kart. At last I waved and he came over. "Great day for outdoor work," says I. "Can I ask you something in a nice way? Can I ask you something simple like one gentleman to another?" Shoot. "Will you get rid of this corn patch? Flowers I have nothing against, but you'll agree I got twenty-four thousand dollars invested in a home, I've got a right to protect it." "I'll share the sweetcorn with you. Would you and your wife come to a corn roast? I'm thinking of building a barbecue, would you like to help?" He affirms that he has tried to reason with me, now warns he will go about it in a different manner since I only want trouble. Do I need trouble, Father Hogan?

How is the work going on the dormitory? I looked around at my corn, the small green tomatoes, climbing beans, remembered the Indian children afraid to eat your school's hot lunch because they never have lunch at home, afraid to eat today because tomorrow they'll be hungry again. I checked out a book on bricklaying yesterday. My wife doesn't understand at all.

My supervisor approaches, the steno at his side. He is grim, puzzled. She wrings her hands. Must close.

In haste,
Haskell

July 27th

Fr. Cyprian Hogan, OFM
Cheyenne Mission School
Broadaxe, Montana

Dear Fr. Cyprian:

Telephoned home this afternoon. "Any mail?" I asked my wife. "Where are you calling from?" "Work, where else?" "I thought you weren't supposed to make personal calls." "What mail?" "There's one." "Are you trying to make me angry? One from where?" "Postmarked Montana." "Bring it down, I'll meet you in the parking lot." "I've got better things to do with my time." Name one, I said, but she wouldn't, so I had to wait to get home this evening to write you.

I am honestly excited about the possibilities of the new industry as a means of helping the Cheyenne. My professional opinion of the full-color brochure layouts on the jewelry you're making is no less than good. Good. If you want I'll show them to the art boys at work and pass their judgment along. How are the orders coming in?

After sound and fury, my wife agrees to telephone all her friends and drum up a big sale for you. "How?" she says. "Have a party, I'll get out of the house, the way they do for pots and pans." Tomorrow she promises to start.

At first I pondered: Indian jewelry? But *what* doesn't matter, I see now. *Why* is all. You start with fifteen employed—how soon can you expand? You make mail order jewelry in order to remake men; I sell air conditioners. The check's only ten again, but I'll nag my wife to come up with an order for the beads that will more than make up for it.

I appreciated the personal note. Was my letter "diffuse"? It was one of those days. That set my wife off again. Am I writing letters on the sly now? I write because I need to write, I feel like writing. Am I going into the charity business? I give because I want to give. She just doesn't understand, does she. All's well now though; I agreed to go visit my brother and his wife with her.

One failure: I tried to ship you some corn and beans I harvested this week (I knew tomatoes would never make it). "Can't take it," said the little man in the blue coat at the post office. "It'd spoil." I might have said: what good's a post office that can't ship food from one man to another? People are starving out there! But he looked tired, and his blue jacket was wrinkled. Will two wrongs make a right?

Your friend,
H. Haskell

P.S. Are summers in Montana such you could use an air conditioner in the school or the new dormitory when it's done? I might be able to start something at the office to get them to contribute one. Isn't it deductible?

August 14th

Dear Father:

No letterhead stationery this time. I'm not at work, but that's all arranged. I couldn't do what I was supposed to. The steno did her best, didn't sic the supervisor on me for some time. "Mr. Haskell," she said, "if you don't give me that stuff then I've got nothing to do and Miss Lubin will be after me for sitting around." No small thing, Miss Lubin is huge and acne-scarred. What could I do. "Maybe later," says I. "Not now." She had to bring my supervisor. His name is Knauer; all my copy has to go through him.

"What is it you think you're doing, Haskell?" "I told him

I hadda have that stuff or Miss Lubin gets after me, Mr. Knauer," the steno said. I think she was beginning to enjoy it. "I'll do this," Knauer said. The typewriters slowed down on the other side of the glass; there hadn't been any excitement in the office since personnel hired a mousey girl named Peplinski (her name I knew!) months ago—she was a secret epileptic and threw a fit at her desk, chewed right through some bond paper one afternoon. "I can't do anything," I said.

"Are you ill, Haskell? Are you trying to pull something off on me?" "The Indians need me, Knauer," and I might have gotten snotty with him, but remembered that everyone calls him Weasel Knauer behind his back because of his narrow pointed face, so took pity and kept silence. "He's been talking funny about those Indians," he whispered to the steno, and they backed out afraid. He came back with a janitor to protect him in case I raged. "You can feel free to go home if something's wrong, Haskell," he said. The janitor carried a long-handled broom to subdue me. Am I the violent type? "Just till you feel better. Don't worry about a thing," he said, "I'll contact personnel for you."

"I'm worried about the Indians, Weasel Knauer," I said, but he kept on backing out to make sure the janitor was between us until I left the office. The girls in the steno pool tried not to stare.

My wife won't know about this letter either because she hasn't been here for three days. It could be she calls, or it could be personnel wanting to know if I'm terminating, but I don't answer the phone. I came home like they told me at the office, and I could talk to her, but she didn't quite understand.

"I'm telling you why if you'll listen to me. It was the Indians. I couldn't do what I'm supposed to do there," I said.

Said she: "I don't know what's the matter with you, you talk about the Indians all the time. You never say anything except about the Indians all the time. Stay over there. Don't touch me. I don't understand you anymore. I don't want to talk about the Indians anymore." What was there left to say? But I kept on talking, and finally she cried, and she cried, so I stopped for good. So she left. I think she's with my brother and his wife. Her parents live far from here. The phone rings often, and there was someone at the door yesterday and today. I thought I recognized the broken muffler on my brother's Oldsmobile.

Why don't you write? Are you still waiting for that jewelry order I promised? Give up, Father. Nobody wants Indian-style jewelry, not my wife, not anybody. She broke her promise about holding that party to sell it. "I'd be ashamed to show cheap jewelry like that to my friends." I tried to tell her how it was to help the Cheyenne, but who understands? I think they have all the jewelry they need.

I've thought better of it too, Father. Sending out plastic teepees and Indian dolls, cheap jewelry, that's not the way, not for me anyhow. I gave Sitting Bull to the neighbor girl, but her mother brought it back. "Keep your trashy presents to yourself!" she screamed when I opened the door. I was afraid she'd have an attack of some kind. When her husband came home that night he stood in his yard and glared at my cornfield with his hands on his hips. My tomatoes are rotting on the vines. I started with a bushel basket full at the other end of the block to give them away, but when the woman (maybe it was a maid?) peeked through her curtains to see who it was she waved me off. The word must be out on Haskell.

No, the way is things like the mission school, and the free hot lunches for children who don't get them at home, and finding Thomas abandoned in the autowreck. That's the way. Build that dormitory and staff the school with teachers so you can have classes more than half a day. What kind of a world is this?

The doorbell's ringing. Maybe you've written, but I haven't gone out to see the mail. There won't be any money in this letter because my wife took the checkbook with her. I might as well answer the door, I've got to go out to mail this (if I can find a stamp). Money's not the way anyhow.

September 5th

Dear Father:

Here's proof I no longer ignore the mail, though now all my letters are delayed a day or two because of my change of address. I've been with my brother and his family for the past few days. My wife is now with her parents, and while I'm grateful to my brother for taking me in, I will be glad to leave (he is glad our mother didn't live to see this, etc.). My sister-in-law won't stay alone in the same room with me, and their children are with her parents until I go. Can I blame them? Accept, I say to myself, they don't want to understand.

From your letter, Father Hogan, I'd almost think you didn't understand either. I'm satisfied to think that's just a problem caused by my "diffuse" expression. I comment briefly; there's much to do before I can be on my way.

Agreed, the world's as it is because we're like we are. Now concede we can change it by changing ourselves. Proof? Look in the mirror. I'm argument enough for me.

Friends, clergyman, psychiatrists? Come on now! Do I need friends with a brother like mine? I went to church last Sunday—my brother's high Episcopal these days—it's the closest one. "Excuse me, Reverend," I said (my brother says he's called Father, like you). "Would you read this little prayer and appeal for the northern Cheyenne at the end of your sermon for me today? I've got my telephone number right there if anyone wants to call in a pledge." I still have the mark on my arm where my brother grabbed me when he pulled me away to a pew. "Can't I even let you out of the house?" he said. You're the only clergy I know, and I've been consulting, not your letters, but your example. I don't see doctors because I don't have money (that's all my wife's: house, car, our small savings)—what do I need money for? I know the language of psychiatrists. They don't want to change the world.

Here I am then. We can talk all this over in detail later if you want. I wish I could say exactly when, but there are papers to be signed, arrangements—I hope for the best. Who knows, with luck I might arrive at the mission shortly after this letter.

You'll see, I'll be of use. I'll mix cement, lay bricks, teach school. I'll scour the mountains for abandoned children. I can learn. I haven't told you before this because I feared you wouldn't understand. But you'll see. It may take longer than I think. I have so little money I may have to hitchhike all the way to Montana. What does time matter when you've found your way at last, Father?

My brother shouts from downstairs that dinner is ready. The flesh must be fed. I'll close:

H. Haskell, Your Friend in Christ.

# NIGGER SUNDAY

FOR SUDS, the nigger, Sunday was the best day, and always had been. When he was a little boy, he spent the summer days collecting scrap metal in a coaster wagon, selling what he had collected to the Jew dealer, and hoarding his money for Sunday, when he would get up early and dress in his best clothes and take a bus downtown, where the movies cost half a dollar for children.

He would go to the big theater with carpets in the lobby as soon as it was open, and stay there until late at night, watching the first-run feature over and over from the balcony, going down to the lobby to buy things to eat every time the newsreel came on. He always made it back to the balcony in time for the previews, so he would know what he would be seeing the next Sunday. His favorites were westerns and spy stories.

When he got home from downtown, very late, his mother would scold him, and then he would lie in bed, staying awake and feeling let down, not wanting Sunday to end, and thinking that it had gone by too fast, leaving him tired and disappointed. Worst of all was knowing that he would have to get up early and go out with his coaster wagon and get something to sell to the Jew so he could go downtown again next Sunday. He didn't think then that he liked living very much.

Growing up had not changed him. He worked on Saturdays at the car wash until six, and then he went with the other washers for a few beers, but he came home early and went right to bed, happy with his life on Saturday nights, for he would be rested when he awoke early Sunday, and he would still have money to spend all day.

Suds was a good son. He gave his mother money for living at home. He only kept enough for new clothes once in a while, and busfare and smokes for the week, but he always kept out a special amount for Sunday. The first thing he counted out of his pay on Saturday was enough for him to blow on Sunday. That came first.

The sun, through his window, promised a fine Sunday as Suds carefully dressed. The careful dressing was important to the day. He put his hat on, turning the brim down all the way around, and looked in his mirror, singing to himself.

"Oh Lord my boy Suds it's Sunday yes it's Sunday, oh yes Lord, my sweet boy Suds, it's one good goddamn fine ding dong daddy Sunday!" He chuckled at having been able to think of such good words for the same tune as *Long John,* which was his favorite song, and then he rubbed at his moustache and goatee.

Once he had told a woman that he was a horn player and so didn't dare to shave too near his mouth for fear of cutting his lip, and she had believed it for a while. He chuckled.

Finished dressing, clean and pressed all over, he checked himself in the mirror for the final time, was pleased, and then hurried outside.

It was warm, and there were already a few people on the street. He looked at their clothes and decided that his Sunday rags were about as keen as any. He smiled and stretched, and then did a little step on the sidewalk. A whole Sunday.

On Sunday, he was happy with his life, and liked his job

at the car wash. He felt that it was possibly too good. It was Sunday, and it had only started, and the whole thing was still before him. He was right in it, he could reach right out and there it was, all day. He paused for an instant before starting it off. He did another little step for the whole thing, and then he started it.

He crossed the street and went to The Bronzeville Bar. He said hello to Bugs and a couple of fellows who had started drinking already. No sir, not for him, that was how to ruin a Sunday. The Bronzeville always smelled good, a Sunday smell when everyone was dressed keen, and everyone bought plenty of drinks instead of nursing, and all the men smoked cigars.

He bought a handful of eight-cent cigars, being sure just to fill his hand when Bugs opened the box for him, making sure not to count how many he took, but just reaching in and taking as many as his hand could hold gently, so that none of them were broken and wouldn't smoke right. That was Suds's Sunday way of buying cigars.

The Bronzeville was surely a good place. Just one then, one beer before going back out on the street to really get into Sunday. Bugs gave him the beer, and Suds lit his first cigar after carefully arranging them all in his breast pocket so the bands would show. When he smoked a cigar on Sunday, he always left the band on.

With the beer and the cigar—so good so good—he decided to play *Long John* once before leaving. He'd had Bugs give him plenty of dimes—he played *Long John* often on Sunday. He drank the beer slow, so he would finish just as the record was done playing. So good.

He went back out on the street. He took his Sunday place on the corner, putting his hands in his pockets, just far enough in so that his cuffs stood out and showed his keen links. He kept the cigar with the band on in his mouth, puffing on it and making it glow a little whenever a girl passed close to him.

Suds watched the girls come out to walk. The girls always walked, and the other fellows, like Suds, stood and watched them. They checked for how keen their Sunday rags were, and they checked to see if any girls stopped walking to talk to any of the men.

Shortly, a couple of men joined Suds at his corner place, and they talked in the Sunday way, which is something like on the other days, but is different because they were really talking about how it would be, and not about something already over, which is never as good. Sunday is the only day they talked like that.

"I was high, what I mean is you better know I was high. You better know it and believe it that I was high," said one.

"Well you better know it and believe it that I'm gone be high," Suds said, doing his little step.

"Oh, hey, look at Suds, look at him, I say look at him, will you looky, one time!" said another, and they all laughed and continued talking in the Sunday way.

Suds watched the girls and checked what rags people were wearing. He watched Coleman's gas station, and saw, with professional interest, the washers on the job. He'd never work there, because they worked on Sunday morning. He lit another cigar, leaving the band on, and it was as good as the first. Here it was Sunday, he thought, and still in the morning, and the whole rest of it still to go.

All week long, live for that Sunday, and know it and see it coming and here it is, still in the morning with every bit of it fine, and the whole way still to go. So good, so good to be right on it!

At just the right time, Napoleon picked him up in his convertible, and they went to cruise the beach. On Sunday, he and his friend always cruised before Napoleon went to pick his woman up.

They laughed and told each other how keen their rags were. Down at the beach, they checked all the girls they passed, and sometimes Napoleon would sound his wolf horn at them, and the girls would look at them, and Suds would wave, holding his cigar in his teeth. It was good doing that. The tailpipes fluttered when Napoleon zoomed past the girls, and the girls would giggle.

"And I told her, if this ain't the first time, then it is the last time, the . . . last . . . time," Napoleon said.

Suds laughed. "Know that, man, know that and believe it!"

Napoleon dropped him off at The Bronzeville when it was time to get his woman. Suds would have liked then to have a woman, especially for Sundays. He ate ribs in The Bronzeville, which is all he ever ate on Sundays. Bugs's wife could make ribs like there was nowhere else on Sundays. While he ate ribs, he had a few more beers and listened to *Long John* twice.

After he ate, Suds went back out on the corner for the last time each Sunday. He did another step for his happiness and his full stomach, and the whole evening and night to come. There were still people on the street, so he checked them, smoking another cigar. It was so good after the ribs. He let smoke flow out his nose, and blew it some down over his chin, and then pursed his lips and streamed it up high. So good.

It nagged him a little to think some of Sunday was gone, but there was still plenty to go, and what was gone was still fresh in his mind, and he was right in the middle of it.

All week, all week, and it was here. It was so good to think of it coming all week, and then wake up, and there it was, you were right in it! Suds blew out lots of that good smoke and chuckled. The morning had gone fast, but there was plenty more.

He went into The Bronzeville again and started playing *Long John*. Then he went to the bar and drank beer. He never drank booze, because his money would run out too soon, and he would get drunk too fast. He liked to get high very gradually on Sunday, so that he could keep feeling the good feeling of being high grow on him.

When he had enough beer to feel confident, he went over to the pool table and picked up the rack to challenge the winner. They played for games and beers, and sometimes Suds played very well and got a lot of free beer.

If the game was going okay for him, he would talk his pool talk, and some of the fellows at the bar would watch him shoot. He would take off his coat and roll his sleeves up, and with his cigar at an angle in his mouth he would shoot with the smoke drifting up to the table light and making him squint. He thought this made him look almost like a regular sharker sighting along the cue.

"Better put some draws on that one," somebody would tell him.

"No," Suds would say, chalking up. "Don't need no draws on that one; what I need on that one is some legs."

"Man, you nothing but hustled on that one!"

"Man," Suds would say after the shot, "I had to hustle on that one!"

They were falling good for him, so he talked Bugs into coming out behind the bar and shooting him nine-ball for a dollar, and he almost won. He laughed when he paid Bugs the dollar, because he knew Bugs could take anybody on his own table.

This hurt him for money a little, though, and he got a little cold when he saw by the clock how late it was already. The Sunday was running out fast, even though it still was, he was still in it, and he could remember the whole day just fine.

He drank some more to get back with it, and thought how this was what he was looking forward to all week while he washed cars, and here it was, and he was having one good time, so good. He still like his life, and the Sunday was still as good as when he was a boy, and he still liked his job that paid every Saturday so that he was ready for his day.

Napoleon came in with his woman, and Suds bought for them so that they would stay and he would be able to enjoy it, and forget how the time was running.

Napoleon's woman was looking good, which made Suds think again of a girl for Sundays, and he wondered if maybe she liked him any. He gave Napoleon a cigar and bought for them some more so they wouldn't think of leaving.

"That's going to be a bad day tomorrow, man, my head is going to be bad," Napoleon said.

"No, come on, man, don't say so, this is Sunday, this the day you supposed to live!" Suds said.

He checked the clock and saw how late it was, and he got a little scared to see that the crowd in The Bronzeville was thinning, and Bugs was just sitting behind the bar instead of going around talking to the people.

He played *Long John* again, and even sang along with it some, and bought for Napoleon and his woman, and for Bugs too, so it would wake up a little, but they kept on leaving, and finally Napoleon left with his woman.

Finally, he was alone with Bugs, who was cleaning glasses and turning off the bar lights and the pool table light. He had another beer and played *Long John* again, but he knew he'd have to go soon, and there was nowhere for him to go but home because he was nearly broke.

"I'll see you, huh, Bugs?" he said.

"Yeah, don't work too hard, hear?" Bugs said.

He'd be damned if he would even think about working at all, he decided as he went outside. The street was empty, and it had become chilly, but it was still a nice Sunday night . . . no, it was Monday morning already.

He pulled out his last cigar and lit it with the band still on. He puffed, blowing smoke and wondering if it tasted good when he heard something. Down the block a little, Napoleon and his woman were laughing and fooling around some in the convertible. Suds couldn't see much in the dark. Then Napoleon started the car and it fluttered away.

Suds walked toward his house, wanting a woman for Sundays, and wishing he had a car, and knowing that it was over; wanting and wishing and knowing.

He'd looked forward to it, and knew sure it was coming all week, and now the whole damn thing was over already. His money was all spent, The Bronzeville was closed, and nobody was on the street. He hated his life now, and he hated his work.

There was nothing now but to work all week. He waited for it all week, and what the hell was it? It went by like lightning, and it was gone, and there was nothing but waiting again, and then it would zip by again, and there was nothing but working at the car wash.

The beer in his stomach had gone bad, and when he got to his front door he felt the cigar making him sick. He dropped it and ground it out, but it was too late. He hurried over to the gutter and vomited. As he coughed and spat, he hated living, hated Sunday. It was nothing.

On Monday morning, when Suds's mother woke him up

in time for work, he very nearly did not go. He could have stayed in bed, slept, then spent the day in the house, maybe gone to The Bronzeville and cadged some beers on credit. His mouth was sour from vomiting, and in the chair where he had thrown them when he went to bed, his keen Sunday rags were all wrinkled. He looked at them dimly through his half-sleep for a time, and then got up and dressed for work.

He'd have to leave them at the cleaners if he wanted them for next Sunday, because he could already feel it and know it coming.

# 1 FANTASTICO

HE WAS NOT CALLED Fantastico—the fantastic one—until after he became a photographer. But for six years he was known by this name to the people of the Ramblas, the wide boulevard that runs nearly the entire length of the city of Barcelona from Franco's summer palace, guarded by mounted lance-bearing Moors, all the way to the harbor, where there is a huge column, a monument that still shows the scars inflicted upon it by the dashing young German of the Condor Legion who strafed the docks one afternoon during the civil war with his *Stuka's* machine gun.

On the Ramblas there are two kinds of people, Spaniards and Americans. The Spaniards include prostitutes, pimps, police, shopkeepers, clerks, vendors, shoeshine boys and men, and Fantastico's landlady. The Americans are all soldiers and sailors, men who have come from England, France, Germany, North Africa, Iceland, and the Atlantic and Mediterranean fleets to the great city of Barcelona in search of pleasure. For six years all these people knew him as Fantastico.

Before this time his name was simply Jorge, and for specific reason neither he nor anyone else in his family made mention of a last name; he was illegitimate. It was a disgrace to his mother and her family, who were freeholders of a small farm. To acknowledge her shame his mother never spoke the family name of his father, and her family refused to grant her son their name. So he was Jorge.

He was born in the family home on the farm outside the city of Figueras in 1929. The village priest baptized him simply Jorge. After the baptism, wine was drunk out of deference to the presence of the priest, but when he left, the men of the family, Jorge's grandfather and uncle, returned to their work in the fields. Three days later his mother was sent to Figueras to live, because the men of the family refused to speak to her, and her mother could not bear the gossip and malice of neighbors who visited often under the pretense of offering consolation to the new grandmother. It was a great shame.

His mother learned to work as a baker's helper in Figueras, and here he lived until he was seven. He found his first work here, shining shoes when *turistas* from France or Madrid, in the south, came through the city and stopped to eat at the sidewalk restaurant or stay overnight in the largest hotel.

When the first cities were bombed during the civil war, the men of the family relented, and there were other topics for gossips then. Jorge and his mother were taken back to the farm. He lived there until he was twenty. His maternal grandparents happened to be in Figueras at open market the day that city was razed. Their bodies were believed to be among those burned in a fire set to the church where many had fled from the attacking Moors. At least they were never found.

His mother cared for the poultry and the household vegetable garden. Jorge assisted his uncle in the fields, picking olives and herding the few livestock. This work he enjoyed. In the middle of a sun-blazing field there was, of course, no one to spit the word *bastardo* at him.

In 1949 his uncle married a girl who had inherited a piece

of land adjacent to the family farm, and this made the uncle dream of expansion, of increasing the family fortune in a way that would do honor to the memory of his murdered parents. He purchased a breeding bull. Jorge's mother walked into the bull's paddock by mistake and was trampled to death. Jorge sensed that the tie of his welcome had been cut.

"Tell me," he said to his uncle, "what you think of my leaving here."

"Leaving for where? To go where?"

"To anyplace. To Figueras perhaps."

"Why would you want to leave? You can stay if you like." As he spoke his uncle was busy trimming a stick to use as a goad on his livestock. He did not look at his nephew's face.

"What is there here for me?"

"What is there anywhere for you? Work. Food to eat. A roof to sleep under. How much does anyone need?"

"But I mean finally. What is there here that belongs to me?"

"I will have children of my own," said his uncle, and shrugged. He tried the finished goad, cutting the air with it and clucking as he would at the cattle he intended to drive before him.

"Then I'm going."

"I only ask two things of you," said his uncle, squinting along the shaft on the stick. "If you go, please go farther than to Figueras. Otherwise it will look as if I sent you away. And this isn't so."

"What else?"

"Please don't call yourself by my name. My name is a good name, and with the death of my sister, people's memories will be short."

The next city of opportunity after Figueras was Barcelona.

To the north were only mountains, and he had no wish to leave Spain. So he walked to Figueras and obtained a labor permit to travel south.

"Age?" the clerk asked.

"Twenty."

"Occupation?"

"Occupation?"

"Yes, occupation. You wish a permit for work. What kind of work do you do?"

"I've worked on a farm."

"There are no farms in Barcelona. It has to state some work you can find in Barcelona if you want the permit for there. Can you do anything else?"

"I shined shoes for *turistas* here in Figueras when I was seven."

"Shoeshine boy then," said the clerk, and validated the permit with his seal. "Keep away from whores," he advised. "You'll do better in a place like Barcelona if you remember that."

He never shined shoes. The Ramblas was already filled with men twice his age, dressed in studded jackets and tasseled caps, carrying big cases of shoeshine gear on straps over their shoulders. Nor did he watch parked cars. That was done by disabled veterans of Franco's army who still wore their combat tunics and greatcoats. He was tempted to beg, but the only ones who did well at this were very old or disfigured by disease. Jorge had severe acne, but this was not enough.

An employment agency found him work as a kitchen helper for a mortgage on half his first year's salary. He worked fourteen hours a day at the nightclub *Gardenias Granada,* and here he learned to speak conversational English because all busboys and waiters and kitchen helpers studied English and practiced it together. Here, too, he learned the art of photography.

One could advance if one was diligent, polite, quick, efficient, and hygienic at all times when on duty. In three years he advanced from kitchen helper to dishwasher, and in two more, because he broke no dishes and was hygienic and had learned English quickly, to waiter's assistant. Perhaps five years more would have seen him a waiter; a waiter could earn enough to marry, for example. Perhaps by the time he was forty-five he would have been established, with no reason to envy his legitimate cousins, who were heirs to the freehold near Figueras.

But in November of 1955 he met Foto Joe, the German, who was on vacation. Foto Joe wore a thick wool suit with a vest. He had a wristwatch, a diamond and onyx ring on the little finger of his left hand, and smelled agreeably of barber's lotion. He sat at the bar with cigarette case and lighter next to his ashtray, playing with a rum drink between his palms when Jorge walked by. It was too early for the music, too early yet for the hostesses to make their appearance, so few customers were in the barroom. But Piaf was singing at *Gardenias Granada* for a month beginning that night, so there were things to be checked at the waiters' station in readiness for the huge crowds expected.

"Hey kiddo," said Foto Joe, waving him over with a raised forefinger—on this there was an amethyst ring stuck just on the oversize knuckle—"can you speak English? *Gut.* Come here for one minute please. Come on, I buy you a drink if you want."

"I'm not allowed to drink, sir," Jorge said.

"Then tell me a few things. You have a minute, okay? Who takes in here the pictures?"

"Pictures?"

"*Ja,* pictures. Who has the concession? I was here all last night by the bar, no one I see taking pictures. No photographer here? One hell the waste. He could make a fortune." Jorge took time to listen.

Foto Joe was originally from Munich, but now lived in Murnau, where the U.S. Army had an Engineer school. He did straight commercial photography, too, but the money was in the yearbooks he did. He laughed when he called them six-weeks books. With each new class of soldiers that shipped in for the six-week course he made his pitch. He would personally take pictures of them in all the activities they engaged in at school—getting fed in the mess hall, sitting in class, standing inspections in ranks and barracks, marching in formation, and, of course, being handed the diploma by the commandant of the school upon successful completion of the course.

"The reason I stayed in Murnau is I was there in the war in air reconnaissance . . . you know what means that, reconnaissance? . . . that's taking pictures from airplanes. I never was in a airplane, but I learned to use the camera. I married a woman from Murnau too, but she's not on this holiday with me. I send her to Nice next spring if she wants to go away someplace. And let me tell you it don't matter even if the GI don't graduate proper. No sweat. Everybody graduates with Foto Joe. They buy them books like souvenirs to send home to America. You know what's a souvenir?"

Jorge got permission from the captain of waiters to talk to Foto Joe for a while longer. He stood next to him at the bar, and the German gave him an American cigarette from his case.

"What do you need for this business to be a photographer? How much money must I have?"

"Need? A camera is what you need. A good reliable camera, a Retina maybe, that's maybe 170 *Deutschmark,* that's how much your money . . . say about 2,000 *pesetas,* but don't forget you get a deal if you make contract to buy film and get prints all at the same place. Then you get a deal on a Retina I bet you for 2,000 *pesetas,* maybe less. And you don't need no junk on that camera—"

"Junk?"

"That's stuff you don't need. Extra things. Here. See?" He showed him an oversized business card. *Best Wishes From Foto Joe!* it said on the left-hand side, and on the right a picture of the man kneeling, holding a large press camera with flash attachment. Joe was smiling, and from his neck and arms dangled more flashguns, light meters, smaller cameras, and two gadget bags of soft leather. "That's junk. All that stuff. You learn to use your lens and you take pictures down in hell if you want."

"It seems a good business," Jorge said.

"Look at me," said Foto Joe, patting his stomach beneath the vest. "I go from here tomorrow to Madrid. Later I go to Majorca. If I feel like it, I go to England on the way back. I never got there in the war." And he laughed, ordered another drink, switching from rum to French cognac this time, offering his cigarettes to Jorge again.

A year later Jorge went into business and became Fantastico. He never did as well as Foto Joe, because they wouldn't let him work the nightclubs like *Gardenias Granada,* though *Gardenias Granada* hired a woman to take pictures of the customers in 1957; she also was from Germany. But there were other places. There was all the Ramblas. It wasn't the same as Murnau; he had to tip the bartenders in all the places where the soldiers and sailors came to meet the prostitutes, and he had to tip the *Guardia Civil* who patrolled the Ramblas. At the Dancing *Colon,* a good place for pictures of prostitutes hugging and dancing with soldiers, he had to tip Mike Taverner, the doorman who pimped for more than a dozen girls and had been deported from America for white slavery in 1937.

It was because of Mike—*Miguel Taverner* on the cards giving phone numbers he handed out to every customer when they came in, unless the customer was obviously not interested in the girls but going to see the *jai alai* matches on the second floor and maybe place a few bets—that he became Fantastico during the first year of his career as a camera artist.

"Hello Mike," he said, and reached out to give him a fifty *peseta* note as he entered.

"Forget that, old friend," Mike said. "I got somebody wants to talk to you."

"Who wants to talk to me? Who?"

"Friend of mine, too." Mike coughed on his cigar. "Just go inside and you'll see her waiting for you at the bar. A very pretty lady."

"I have no business with ladies." Again he tried to slip the bill to him.

"Forget that. It's free tonight for you," and he turned away to yell greetings to two white-clad American sailors; the fleet was in port and prices had gone up all over town. The woman waiting for Fantastico was a prostitute he'd seen before. She was turning away a petty officer second class when he reached her.

"It's costing you and me both money for me to wait so long for you," she said. She was a little older than most of them, but not yet thirty.

"I didn't ask anyone to wait for me."

"You'll be glad you came. I've got a business proposition for you."

"I'm not interested in your kind of proposition."

"Don't be insulting. And give me a light for my cigarette; it's good manners." He found matches and handed them to her. "Are you interested in money?"

"Sometimes."

"That's funny. Just listen. I can help you make a lot of it."

"How."

"You help me. I help you. You get to nearly everyplace on the Ramblas except the big places, and I don't care about them. If I could dance with *casteñetas,* I'd be in one of the big places, but I can't so I don't worry about them. In my business—" she smiled, "I don't have time to get everyplace anyhow. Not even enough places to really count. And the competition is hard when you're on your own with no friends to help." She looked out over the floor of the Dancing *Colon,* where it was still early enough that the prostitutes outnumbered the Americans to the extent that some tables held three and four girls, combing their hair, checking makeup in mirrors, talking like respectable women at lunch in polite cafés.

"You want me to run for you. I won't. I just take pictures, I don't make arrangements for anyone. Taverner put you up to this. How much does he get?"

"What do you care? I'm saying to you that you'll get more than enough to pay you for your work. All you need to know is a telephone number—I have a friend who has his own taxi. He's a country boy. Like you I think. Aren't you from the country? I'm surprised you never tried to fix yourself up with something before this."

"I haven't and I won't. If I come from the country, that's my affair. I just take pictures."

"Are you joking, or insulting me? I don't think it's so funny."

"Neither do I. I don't want that kind of work. For my own reasons. I take pictures; that's enough for me."

"You're fantastic!" she said, and began to laugh. She went outside and told Mike Taverner. Jorge looked for work in the Dancing *Colon,* but it was too early, so he left soon for the Texas Bar down the street, in the inner patio.

"Hey Fantastico," Taverner said as he left, "You know what they'd call you in Pittsburgh where I lived twenty-two years? *Sucker* is the word. They should have *sucker* in the language here. So long, Fantastico."

"So long," he said, "and don't forget when I come back tonight, later, that I offered you the money."

"Tonight you come in free, Fantastico," said Mike, "anybody so fantastic—anybody so big a sucker gets one night free at the Dancing *Colon* from Miguel Taverner." He laughed and coughed on the butt of his cigar.

Mike Taverner and the prostitute in search of a pimp told the story to other prostitutes. The prostitutes told the story to the bartenders, cooks, and waiters on the Ramblas, and they told it to the shopkeepers and clerks of the street, and they told it to the municipal police and the men of the *Guardia Civil* patrols. When he moved to a better room, one on the third floor of a building just off the Ramblas, in 1958, the concierge knew him.

"Oh," she said, "You're Fantastico. I know you. If I knew before it was you, I would have asked for more money."

"Why?"

"Because everyone knows that Fantastico is a man with good income. Here is your key, this one to the front door until ten. After ten I change the lock, and the watchman lets you in. This one to your room. And please to read the rules of this house posted in the toilet and in the hallway on your floor."

"My hours are late," he said.

"Of course," she said. "You are Fantastico."

For a short time he was much discussed on the Ramblas.

He passed the alcove of the motion picture theater on his way to the barber's where he was undergoing a series of electronic treatments for his acne. In the alcove the vendor of fried fish, squid, chicken, and corn tamales made a point of greeting him. "Hello Fantastico," he called around the hand-rolled cigarette in his mouth, and waved with his long fork. Fantastico nodded and passed, and the vendor ignored the two small capons frying on his charcoal grill to watch him. He watched until his eyes watered from the smoke drifting up into them. He spat the burning stub onto the tile floor and stepped on it.

Fantastico passed a corporal of the *Guardia Civil* just beginning his rounds, very correct and brushed looking in his gray tunic, the lacquered black leather of his hat, belt, holster, and boots reflecting highlights from the sun. "Fantastico," he muttered officially, and the photographer smiled, showing his teeth, and gave the corporal a moderate salute by touching his brow with two relaxed fingers. The corporal stopped to turn and frown after him for a moment, then moved on, stopping in the alcove to speak with the vendor, who sprayed fuel on the charcoal burner in his cart. The capons were taking too long to cook, and soon it would be intermission in the theater.

"That Fantastico, what do you know of him?" the corporal asked.

"Fantastico," said the vendor, wiping two fingers clean on his jaw stubble before rolling another cigarette. "We just now spoke, or rather I spoke to him. That's how it is I know nothing of the man." The vendor looked apologetic, for he was a paid informer.

"He appears to be hiding something," speculated the corporal, checking his moustache in the glass of a poster case.

"I think rather he has nothing to hide, so says nothing,

corporal. You know, of course, of his refusal to pimp for any of the whores?"

"Perhaps his interests are political?"

"Not at all, corporal. I know he is from the country somewhere to the north. He worked at *Gardenias Granada* for several years. Since nearly two years he has taken pictures." The corporal nodded and stroked his cartridge belt.

"What are we to conclude about such a man?"

"We must conclude, in all respect, corporal," said the vendor, taking up his fork from the grill to turn the capons, "that there exist men who are not political, who will not pander, who wish only to take pictures of prostitutes and *Americanos*—all very respectable pictures I add, for I know also that there have been one or two women who offered him a great price to photograph obscenities involving women, men, men and women, women and animals . . ." The corporal raised his eyebrows. "Indeed there have been, and I could supply names to the corporal if he wishes . . ." The corporal signified in the negative; his interests were political. "So we are compelled to conclude that there exist honest, nonpolitical men who wish only to earn a good living with a camera. In short: Fantastico."

The corporal proceeded in a very unsettled mood until he passed a marketing housewife who seemed to glare disrespectfully at his uniform and badges. He halted her, questioned her, and when she failed to behave with enough frightened correctness, searched her market bag for forbidden articles among the vegetables. He was later ashamed for this, but would not confess to himself that his irritation was due to the existence of a nonpolitical photographer.

It was more than a year before Fantastico's behavior was fully accepted. There were other offers to pimp and more offers to photograph obscenities to be refused. The name of Fantastico was applied, remained with him, and finally he himself adopted it.

"My friend," said Thomas the bartender at the Texas Bar where he ate his first meal of each day at four in the afternoons, before the current was turned on in the city and the bars and shops were still lit by tall, cheap dinner candles, "you pay me something each week for the privilege of working in my establishment, correct?" Fantastico, busy building even morsels of steak and egg on his plate, nodded agreement. "This could be changed—reversed, if you wished."

"How so?" he asked, sipping coffee. Thomas leaned over the bar and ran one hand through his hair.

"Very simple. Whenever you photograph a *turista* somewhere else you might give him my card. Also should you meet any soldier who has brought with him to Barcelona a quantity of American whiskey or tobacco, you might inform him of the very high price I pay for these commodities. What do you say to that?"

"You know better than to ask," he said, touching a napkin carefully to his lips. "That I only take pictures—nothing else—is common knowledge on the Ramblas and has been for some time now." Thomas smiled and shook his head.

"I would not call you crazy," he said, "only eccentric."

"I am neither. I am Fantastico." The lights came on, and Thomas hurried to extinguish the candles between two moistened fingertips. Thus, for six years, he was Fantastico.

His workday began at three o'clock in the afternoon when his landlady climbed the stairs to the second-floor landing to awaken him with a yell. She put her feet wide apart and cupped her hands at the sides of her mouth, tipping her head back and calling on the volume she never otherwise required. *"Fan-Tas-Ti-Co!"* she shouted. It echoed in the stairwell, and in moments brought a muffled reply. Once a tenant, a retired man of seventy who still wore his *Falange* beret daily, complained of this.

"Who is this privileged individual who receives such attention?" he asked, his head, bare at this moment, sticking out his door. "And if he is so special, why not walk up another flight and knock on his door?"

"Shut your mouth," said the landlady, listening for Fantastico's answering voice. "Find another building if you don't like this one."

"I am a member in good standing of the *Falange,*" said the man.

"Take the *Falange* to hell with you when you die." When she heard Fantastico's cry she clumped back down the stairs in her loose slippers after once looking out the landing window to see the shopkeepers pushing aside their metal shutters and the vendors relighting their braziers after the *siesta.*

Remembering Foto Joe's picture hung with cameras and accessories, Fantastico developed a distinctive dress. He wore, in all weather, a light black turtleneck sweater, a gray sportcoat, black slacks, and two-tone black-on-white shoes. Of course, his camera and supplies were carried in a soft leather gadget bag slung over one shoulder. Also he wore a simple gold cross on a fine chain in view on the outside of his sweater, but this was not unusual; even the prostitutes wore crucifixes.

Exchanging greetings with his landlady, he entered the Ramblas, crossed it, dodging the hordes of yellow-green taxis, and entered the high arched doorway cut into the face of a tall stone office building. In the inner patio he descended steep steps to the Texas Bar to eat breakfast of steak, eggs, and two cups of half-half coffee and real cream.

If it was Friday he ate fish instead, and there were additional rituals.

On Friday he added a large tip, for Thomas, to the price of his meal. He then climbed the steps to the patio and waited on a bench near the pool in which swam enormous goldfish, shaded by the fruitless palm trees and by the dark glasses he also now affected. The corporal of the *Guardia Civil* met him here shortly to receive his payment. Then he reentered the Ramblas and went to the barber for an electric treatment, the barber passing a glass rod that snapped and spat current over his face. His acne cleared up before he was thirty, but he continued the treatments because they relaxed him and because the barber warned him that, like syphilis, acne could erupt again at any time.

By six o'clock he was at work. He made the rounds of every bar and restaurant where the Americans could be found eatings, drinking, and meeting prostitutes. He was always greeted loudly by them, waiters and waitresses, bartenders, prostitutes and their customers. *"Ai-yah,* Fantastico!" they would scream.

"There's Fantastico. Invite him to have a drink with us."

"Where have you been, Fantastico. I think you're late tonight."

"Fantastico, my lover wants a picture of me to take back to Algeria with him!"

"Fantastico, take one picture of the six of us, but we want two prints each. Don't forget to write that on the slip—twelve pictures for Dona and her friends."

He developed a style. When he walked in, his face was blankly impassive. At the first words, he spread his lips to show his even white teeth. He flexed the skin around his eyes to make them sparkle blackly, and once a sailor told him he looked like Professor Jerry Colona, a famous American. He lifted both arms, palms out, as if to resist an affectionate assault, fingers extended. Removing his camera, he urged his subjects closer together by means of hand motions and facial grimaces. "Remain so," he would say, and whether they smiled or not he told them to smile, and demonstrated the expression himself until the prostitutes choked with laughter, their customers snuggled close to them and smirked, and the bartenders and waiters and waitresses looked on as if in love with the man, his camera, and his creations.

"When can we get the pictures, Fantastico?" the Americans asked.

"You will see me tomorrow," he announced, as if he intended to come upon them wrapped in a mist, materializing only at his own pleasure. Payment was in advance, thirty *pesetas* per print, and the buyer was handed a receipt bearing a number and the inscription *By Fantastico*. He handed the slip over delicately, like it was a dead mouse he held by the tail.

Customers had, literally, to see him for delivery. He recognized some of them, but waited for them to approach him and request their photos. Usually he stopped at the bar for a small tumbler of Spanish brandy and a cigarette. "You got my pictures, Fantastico?" they asked.

"Ah yes, certainly, yes certainly, yes indeed," and he thumbed through a compartment in his gadget bag until he located the matching numbers. These he produced with a flourish, as though his hand were an elegant platter. He watched while the customer inspected the prints, and said, "Nice, yes?" or "Lovely, I think." On the back of each print was his name and the date, stamped in purple ink.

So it went throughout the night, from bar to bar. He was very popular and his work was everywhere to be seen.

In each bar, sometimes above the backbar, pasted and taped to the mirror, sometimes on felt-covered cork bulletin boards, sometimes on wall panels set aside for this purpose, there was a gallery of his photos, pictures unclaimed by their owners. There was little variety in them. Couples in the pictures sat cheek to cheek at tables filled with glasses, bottles, and open packages of cigarettes. Groups of six and eight raised their drinks in toast to the camera's eye. Prostitutes were posed in imitation of movie stars, bosoms thrust up and out, in doorways. The quality of the pictures was not unusual, but the lighting was balanced; it was obvious that whether or not it was a great thing to do, this taking of pictures, Fantastico did it with some competence.

The last stop on his rounds was the open front bar and grill on the Ramblas called the Snack Bar. Here at four in the morning the prostitutes who had made a late connection for the rest of the night brought their customers for a sobering cup of coffee or a light early breakfast eaten standing up at a Formica counter. Here also gathered the few prostitutes who failed to find someone to take them to a hotel where they could get five or six hours sleep before checkout time at noon. Such a woman, morose, did not greet him from where she sulked alone on a stool at the short bar.

"*Chica,* you are not very cheerful this morning," said Fantastico.

"Why should I be? I'm hungry and I have a headache and I'm tired and I don't give a goddamn."

"And unable to smile."

"Give me a reason for smiling in this miserable life, in this miserable city."

"Why, because you are about to eat breakfast here and now with Fantastico. To how many women does this good fortune occur? Robert!" he called to the bartender-cook, "come and take our order for breakfast, and for the love of God be quick, so this forlorn woman will smile at me again." He knew the girl only slightly; she told Americans her name was Dolores, but this was not true. He had not seen her for some time.

"Fantastico, I'm in trouble," she said as they ate. "I've been in jail for days."

"An unpleasant place I'm told. For what?"

"I was accused of stealing a sailor's money. A lie. I was released because he left with his ship. But I'm still in trouble."

"You stole something more?"

"I said it was a lie. I'm a whore and I have done some things I'll always regret, but not steal. I have been refused permission to be on the public streets after midnight without an escort. I don't dare leave here."

"Why have you stayed so late then?"

"I had an escort, a lieutenant who navigates airplanes in Wiesbaden, but the bastard said he was going to the toilet and never returned. And earlier he told me he loved me and wished to take me to live in Wiesbaden with him."

"Bastard is not a nice word."

"If the watchman or *Guardia Civil* find me alone, it means at least a year in jail. They'll shave my head, Fantastico. I'm afraid."

"Then allow me the pleasure of buying you another cup of coffee—Robert, two coffees with real cream if you please—and the honor of escorting you to your door. Fantastico is at your service," and he bowed with a show of his perfect teeth.

On the cobbled street where she lived they waited for the watchman with the keys to the building. They listened to him approaching, his long leaded nightstick measuring the decreasing distance between them in rhythmic taps.

"In a minute you'll be safely asleep. Next time be more careful in your choice of escorts, Dolores."

"Will you come in with me, Fantastico?" She stepped close to him and touched the sleeve of his jacket.

"Do you never cease trying to earn your living?"

"Do you think I would ask you for money, Fantastico? Let's say this night was for love."

"Like the love of the navigator of airplanes?"

"Gratitude then."

"No thank you. I appreciate the distinction you offer me, but no." The watchman was very near now.

"I'm not good enough? You insult me."

"Not at all. I live by wise advice given me many years ago."

"Oh-ho, so it's you, Fantastico," said the watchman. "What are you doing here with this one? I had an idea she'd get herself in trouble right away. Her landlady told me she owes rent, too."

"Are you a collector of rents?" Fantastico said.

"And are you something other than a man who photographs the *putana?"*

"I'm this lady's escort. Open the door as you're paid to do."

"You waste your kindness on her," he said, searching through his keyring.

"I don't think so."

"Goodnight, Fantastico," Dolores said. "You make me ashamed."

"Sleep well."

"Where do you go now? Or are you headed for home yourself, Fantastico?" the watchman asked as he closed and locked the heavy wooden door behind her.

"None of your business. Loyal citizens of Spain need not answer the questions of gossips who carry keys and clubs. Goodnight."

His day's work was over, but he did not go home yet.

He walked, the gadget bag over his shoulder, to the end of the Ramblas, to the foot of the monument defiled by the German *Stuka.* The sun had not yet risen out of the sea to warm the whole length of the Costa Brava into life, but there was a wash of light in the east, a tint of color, and the full-scale replica of Columbus' *Santa Maria* was clearly visible, tugging on its mooring lines in the harbor. He squared his shoulders and lifted his chin to breathe in the air deeply, to wash from his nostrils the scent of Dolores' perfume, and too many American cigarettes and too much Spanish brandy. He cleansed himself of the life of the Ramblas, and the water slapping the dock pilings erased the memory of tavern and dance hall music from his ears.

He tried to remember the streets of Figueras, the voice of his mother, the buck of the plow in his hands in the fields of his uncle's farm, the taste of food grown in the household garden, the smell of a barn and a granary. He laughed at himself—not the styled laugh of Fantastico, but the real laugh of the illegitimate Jorge, who knew only farmer's work and shining shoes of Madrid tourists bound for France across the Pyrenees. Turning to the north he inhaled the wind as if it could carry the smell of home all the way down the eastern coast of Spain.

Shortly after this he received word that his uncle had died, the freehold inherited by his male cousins, and shortly thereafter he met Pilar, who had also come to Barcelona from Figueras.

He was eating in the Texas Bar. Thomas washed glasses and filled the ice bin behind the bar, scratching his thick hair from time to time and remarking to Fantastico that he wished this night were already over. A lone prostitute who called herself Lola picked through the phonograph records on a low table at the opposite end of the barroom, selecting a group to play as soon as the current went on in the city. Pilar entered the red door with three other prostitutes.

"Here's Fantastico!" one shouted.

"Fantastico, take a picture of our friend Pilar."

"Come on, Fantastico, take one picture of all of us for free. Do it for love."

"Fantastico loves nobody, don't you know?" said Lola, a record in one hand, her first rum in the other. "He loves his camera only."

"Be civil," said Thomas. "Let the man eat." He poured coffee for the four who had just arrived. "I wish this day was over," he added.

"Please, Fantastico, one picture of all of us!"

"But I love you all," said Fantastico, "and haven't I always said so?" He took his camera from the stool beside him and still chewing, checked the shutter setting.

"Meet my new friend Pilar," insisted the prostitute called *La Gorda*—the fat one. "She comes from Figueras."

"Figueras?" said Fantastico. "I too come from Figueras."

"I don't believe it," said Thomas. "I think you just exploded one day out on the Ramblas. That's what I think." He laughed by himself and scratched his hair, examined his fingernails.

"I'm from Figueras and once I was a farmer. For thirteen years I was a farmer. I plowed and weeded and milked a cow. This is so." Pilar from Figueras laughed with the others.

"But take the picture, Fantastico," urged *La Gorda.*

"Me too. I want to be in it too," said Lola.

"Then group yourselves, so . . . Lola, stand a bit in front of the fat one or she won't be flattered . . . so. Now smile. Please to smile. See me, how I smile? Ah!" Just before they broke with laughter he tripped the shutter.

"Do I get the picture to keep?" asked Pilar. She was not

more than seventeen, slender, dark of hair and eyes only, with skin so pale that when she came close to him he could see delicate blue veins at her temples. She wore no makeup and smelled as innocent as the sea, as sweet as clean earth. "I would like to keep the picture, Fantastico," she said, "to remember the first day I lived in Barcelona."

"She's a country girl," said Lola. "Does no *puta* live who was born and raised in this stinking town?" She rattled the ice in her glass at Thomas for more rum. "I'm from the stinking country too, near Guernica. To hell with it all."

"Keep talking and you'll be weeping in your drinks," said Thomas. "Go play a record now the light's on."

"Please give me the picture to keep, Fantastico," Pilar said.

"No fair," said *La Gorda*. "If she gets to keep it, what about me? I want one too."

"I'll do better than that," said Fantastico. "I shall bring the print back tomorrow. From our good friend Thomas I shall obtain some tacks. And then"—he pointed to the panel of photos near the door—"I shall display you all, for everyone to see—"

"Oh, I wanted my own copy," said *La Gorda*.

"—but this is better than having your own. Listen. Who knows how long you'll live? Any of you. You die, the picture is lost or discarded. But here"—he widened his black eyes and framed the portrait for them with his thumbs in mid-air—"you live on forever. Imagine the passing of a thousand years—"

"I don't care if I die tomorrow," mumbled Lola. She played "I Ain't Got Nobody," sung by Louis Prima.

"—imagine! In a thousand years you all are dust. Thomas is dust. *La Gorda* is dust—"

"What about you, Fantastico?" asked Thomas. For a moment he was silent.

"That's different. I am Fantastico."

"And when we're dust?"

"You're dust, but your picture remains here on the wall. And you, Pilar, in a thousand years when you are dust, even then some *turista* will come to the Texas Bar for an *apéritif,* and there on the wall he will see you as beautiful as you are today, and may likely lament your death, even then, a thousand years from now."

"Who cares what's going on in a thousand years if you're rotting in the ground?" Lola said, but no one heard her. Thomas was making fresh coffee for everyone, and Louis Prima was still singing loudly. And even if it were quiet, Fantastico would not have heard. He was preoccupied, an unlit cigarette between his fingers, with the immensity of one thousand years, the formlessness of dust, and the fact that though he was Fantastico, he was not in respect to his mortality different from anyone else. Pilar held a match up to him. He thanked her and gave her a Chesterfield from his case in return.

"And what is your name?" he said.

"But you already know—Pilar. Pilar is my name. Didn't you hear before?"

"Really your name? I'm surprised. But then soon it will be something else. No one has a name here for long. Maybe Thomas is really Thomas. Lola is not Lola. *La Gorda* is not *La Gorda.* Someday you will be other than Pilar. Pilar is a nice name; I will be sorry to see you Carmen or Concepción. A pity."

"And you are not Fantastico?"

"Of course not. Who ever heard of such a name. But I'm not the same as them. Look at me, Pilar. I'm past thirty for some time now. And Thomas is also past thirty. Women on the Ramblas are never past thirty. Were it so it would not be the Ramblas."

"Are you trying to save my soul, Fantastico?"

"No. Souls are no joking matter, but I don't save them. Priests do I guess. I only take pictures."

He saw her frequently the next month, sometimes alone, walking on the Ramblas, wearing high-heeled shoes and a raincoat, a few times in the Dancing *Colon* and other bars, in the company of other prostitutes, with soldiers and sailors. Once he saw her enter a taxi with a fat and wealthy looking Spaniard of at least sixty years. Whenever he saw her he was reminded of a thousand years passing silently in stocking feet, and the taste of dust was strong on his tongue, and he remembered that he had no name. He began to confess to a priest and to recite Hail Marys for the repose of his dead mother's soul.

"Good evening, Fantastico!" called the vendor of fish, squid, and tamales. When there was no answer he turned to the corporal of the *Guardia Civil* beside him and said, "Who the hell does he think he is to ignore me?" When the corporal raised his brows he added, "No, corporal, I don't believe he is thinking of politics."

"You're very quiet," said Thomas to him at breakfast. "Would you like me to fix you a powder for your stomach?"

"I'm fine. I wonder, Thomas," he said, "what is there for me here?"

"How do you mean?"

"What is there for me, Fantastico, in the city of Barcelona. What is there for me besides the taking of pictures with a camera. What is there for me to have?"

"I don't understand. You have more money than ten men like me. You're a lucky man, Fantastico."

"What makes you say that?"

"Someday soon—before you're fifty—you'll retire and go live like a gentleman in Madrid." He asked Fantastico to smile, and he did, and the photographer bought Spanish brandy for the two of them.

"I didn't sleep well this morning," said his landlady when he left for the night. "I could hear you walking in your room. Were you ill?"

"Thinking," said Fantastico.

"How can a man so fortunate have anything to worry about?" she asked, and talked to herself much of the early evening about this.

The troopers of the *Guardia Civil* patrols reported to their corporal that he sometimes stood for hours at the docks on the end of the Ramblas, until long after the sun rose, as if waiting for a signal from smugglers in boats, or perhaps political agents. But no signals were observed by the detail assigned to watch him, and the corporal behaved tyrannically for two weeks over this. "Damn his impudent good fortune!" he swore to the vendor, who sympathized and rolled a cigarette for the corporal.

There was more than the considerable money he had on account in postal savings to the good fortune of Fantastico. The people of the Ramblas envied him this, but there was more. When he met them and performed his show of smiles, wide eyes, and raised hands for them, and sometimes did small favors for them, too, they lost their sense of themselves. They forgot momentarily that they were prostitutes or cart vendors or poorly paid policemen. When he left them they remembered who they were, and it made them unhappy to remember. But to forget for a time, though brief, was worth all regret. He was Fantastico because he could not be what he was, and still, they were forced to concede, he was, for there he stood before them to see.

Possibly if Pilar had known him longer, she would not have told the story, but she was no more than seventeen and had only recently come to Barcelona from Figueras to the north.

"Pilar," he called to her where she sat with another girl at a table early one night in the Googi Bar. She joined him at the bar. "So you are still Pilar."

"Still Pilar. And you are still Fantastico?"

"For a short time longer only. Have a drink. I wish to talk to you."

He explained to her that he held a considerable account in postal savings. He told her he was thirty-three years old and had lived in Barcelona for thirteen years. He told her of Foto Joe and the *Gardenias Granada.* He told her of his birth and of the land owned by his family near Figueras. He had communicated with his cousins. They welcomed an investment in the farm, for machinery, more livestock perhaps, options on adjacent land. They welcomed him back to the family. He asked her to marry him and return to Figueras.

"I'm a prostitute," she said when she ceased laughing and wiped the dampness from her eyes with a handkerchief.

"I am aware of that. You are a prostitute. My birth was a disgrace to the name of my mother's family. These things can be forgotten. There is nothing here for either of us. Come with me, Pilar."

"You haven't said you loved me," she joked.

"I have yet to learn to love. I have years left in which to do this. Will you come?"

"Fantastico," she said, "I think you are mad!" and it took several retellings of the story to her friends before they would believe that Fantastico had not been playing an elaborate joke on her. No one had much opportunity to ridicule him to his face.

"I am tired of being Fantastico," he said to her, "and soon

you will be weary of being Pilar. When you die you'll be buried under some cheap whore's name in the potter's field. I pity you."

"Save your pity for your cousins," she laughed. "What will farmers do with a man who knows only the use of a camera!"

"I was once a farmer." He withdrew his savings and returned to the farm. His male cousins, their wives, and children, were there to greet him when he left the train at Figueras. A large party was held to honor him. The village priest was applauded when he drank wine directly from a goatskin, and neighbors came all through the night to see him, slap him on the back and address him familiarly as Jorge.

"Tell us, Jorge," they said, "is everyone rich as you in Barcelona?"

"Forget your city, Jorge," they said smiling. "There's no excitement like that when you break the ground for a living."

"Who knows?" they asked one another. "Maybe this farm will become a large ranch soon. Who knows how much money the little bastard has hidden in his shoe?"

The farm did not become a great ranch, then or ever. And they learned that what money he had was not enough. When machinery was purchased a tax official came from the district office in Figueras and levied a special assessment against the farm. One cousin borrowed 25,000 *pesetas* for the purpose of bidding at a livestock auction, but it turned out he gave some of it to a prostitute in Figueras and spent the rest on lottery tickets. Jorge damaged the new tractor severely by using the wrong gear when trying to uproot a tree stump. He quarrelled with his cousins' wives because they nagged him to know if he planned to leave money to their children in his will. His cousins foisted the most unpleasant work onto his shoulders, berated him for spending money on expensive brandy and cigarettes, and called him *The Bastard* behind his back. In a year his money was gone, and his tie of welcome was broken for the second time.

"I'm getting out of here," he told his oldest cousin. "You've bled me dry."

"Leave then," said his cousin. "No one promised you a soft life here. You come here with a lot of talk and expect to be supported like an old man of wealth. Get off my land. And never use my name; you've no right to it."

"Bloodsuckers," Jorge said to him. "Thief. Brother of thieves, father of thieves."

"Bastard, get out!" and his cousin picked up a heavy length of firewood.

"Name?" said the clerk who filled in his travel permit in Figueras.

"Name?"

"Name. What's your name? That's easy enough isn't it?"

"Fantastico."

"That's no name."

"Jorge then. My name is Jorge."

He returned to Barcelona and again became a photographer. He deposited regularly in an account at the post office. But no one called him Fantastico. When they saw the deep tan on his face, the cracked and split condition of his fingernails, his misshapen shoes stained with dirt and manure, the way he held his kidney when he bent too quickly, they poked one another, laughed, and called him Jorge. Jorge the Farmer. Jorge the Fool. Never Fantastico.

He asked once after Pilar. "Pilar? Go to the *Gardenias Granada*. She's bleached her hair platinum and dances with *casteñetas,* and she'll be a major performer yet. She's damn good and also sleeps with a banker—or maybe he's a government official, I forget which. Someday she'll be famous."

Only Mike Taverner still uses a nickname when Jorge comes to work at the Dancing *Colon*. Mike had a stroke and has to pass out his cards while sitting on a chair and leaning on a cane. "Good evening, Mr. Sucker," he says when he takes the fifty *peseta* note.

# ELEMENTS OF THE 10th MOUNTAIN INFANTRY RECONNOITER

"AREN'T YOU GOING TO at least put on a tie?" his wife said, stepping into the bathroom doorway.

"Never," Hackbarth said. "You don't see the *Gestalt.* Ties are out. As are coats and pants that match, at least if they're too severe." Their eyes meeting in the mirror, his wife shrugged. "This is not a departmental meeting," he said, finger-adjusting the flop of his forelock to a more casual lie. "This is not your ancient and solemn Dean of the College, Yale, class of nineteen and thirty-four. None of your sober and senior members of the faculty. This is not to welcome the visiting poet-lecturer on tour." She stepped out of the doorway, but he continued for her benefit and his own.

"It won't be warm sherry, oh no, not on your life. I venture it's beer, cold enough to crack your teeth, make your temples ache . . ."—he paused to grope for another image, the topper, complete the series, but his own words had taken hold, and he remembered: beer. Beer as it was then, the essence, essential substance, stuff of *beer!*

Once the area was clear of noncoms, the motor pool animals telephoned Graf's. A kraut kid on a bicycle delivered it through the *Kaserne* fence, half-liter brown glass bottles with white porcelain caps, clinking gently and catching the sun, carried in a net bag slung from the handlebars. The motor pool animals set them in a tub, filled it with gasoline up to the necks, stuck the air hose in, and turned it on. Basic refrigeration dynamics: beer so cold it burned your throat all the way down, made your ears ring!

"You were saying?" his wife said from somewhere in the kitchen. Hackbarth blinked, alone in his bathroom.

"Booze," he said. "Hootch. Simple and efficient to the purpose at hand. No warm sherry. None of your chocolate soda Alexanders. No frothy *apéritifs,* no fruit garnish, possibly not even any napkins. No sir. What I'm saying is, basic. Beer, bourbon, gin, vodka, maybe, and if old Red Oates has a touch of style, a penchant for flair, then, possibly, cognac and coke which is as it should be."

"No thank you," his wife called from a distance.

"Suit yourself," he said, closing the bathroom door. He turned on the faucets for cover, and took the photo from his pocket, propped it on the shelf below the mirror, then concentrated on details, scrutinized: comparison and contrast—

What we are doing, ladies and gentlemen, is to take two objects, entities, from the scope of our common or particular reality, observe those qualities, features, points, aspects, which are similar. Hence, we compare. And those which are dissimilar, hence, distinctive. We contrast. Thus, one of the primary techniques by which we achieve exposition, one of the four modes of rhetoric.

Any questions? In his mind's eye, Hackbarth saw the class, bored, staring at their feet or notebooks, the invisible smoke of their prayers for the bell rising to the ceiling.

Very well then, let us proceed.

The photograph was as good as new. Printed on stiff paper, kept carefully over the years between handkerchiefs in his dresser drawer, it had suffered no bend or wrinkle, no crack or discoloration. Hackbarth, in class-A uniform, complete with garrison cap, smiled sardonically with the assuredness of his barely twenty years. It was black and white, but memory supplied the proper tints. Blue infantry braid on the cap, gleaming brass badges, the crossed rifles of the Queen of Battle, gold-brown of his corporal's chevrons, and the alternating red and white stripes of a Good Conduct Ribbon, his sole decoration in three years of peacetime occupation service.

Ah now, he thought. There's our boy! "Looking good, standing tall, straight like six o'clock," he whispered beneath the hiss of the running faucets. "Sharp," he whispered.

Looking up, he forced his face into impassivity, and with resolute honesty surveyed the subtle damage of time.

Contrast: the hairline had crawled back, too far even for the calculated flop of his forelock to conceal. "Father to daughter to half the daughter's sons," he intoned, ultimately safe in the knowledge that his grandfather had died at eighty-four, white, yes, but thick-thatched. Lines, across the forehead, accumulating like pleats in velvet when he lifted his eyebrows. At the outer corner of each eye, small fanlike webs, though barely noticeable, and never when smiling or quizzical. Fair enough. But the sag, a pervasive thing, inflating the jowls slightly, turning his incipient dewlap from shadow to substance, erasing the bone-deep jocularity of the cocky soldier, suggesting a sure suspicion of . . . ennui? Hackbarth dropped his eyes to the gushing water, gripped the edge of the sink, then with a defiant, snapping effort of will, tipped back his head.

"Oh but you got the choppers, though, boy!" he said, and glared at himself in the mirror, lips drawn back to expose his white, even teeth, to the gums. His wife caught him, just that way.

"Narcissus lives," she said, throwing open the door, trying not to smile too much, or too cruelly.

Horribly shamed, he reached for toothpaste and brush. As he brushed, the fire of embarrassment within receded, replaced by deep gratitude, for she had mercifully not pursued, but left almost immediately. By the time he finished, he had achieved the comfort of speculating as to what kinds of dogs his former comrades-in-arms had married.

On his way out, he leaned over his wife to kiss her goodbye. She lowered the newspaper to accommodate him, and Hackbarth saw the faint trace of her smile in her pucker. "Happy television," he said in retaliation, straightening. "How do I look?" he asked, knowing it was a mistake.

"Very nice," she said, and let him have it, "like an assistant professor on a night out with the boys."

"I'm serious. Do I look all right?"

"You look fine," she said, and stopped smiling.

"I mean, the jacket, the hair and everything."

"Just fine. Enjoy yourself," she said.

"I'll be home early."

"You don't have to come home early . . ."

"I mean it," he said, not letting her finish, "I mean, what the hell would I want to stay out all night for? It's just a reunion with some old army buddies."

"Have a good time. You can tell me all about it tomorrow," his wife said, lifting the newspaper. Hackbarth turned to go, but somehow felt it was not yet time, not right.

"You're still welcome," he said. "Their wives'll all be there."

"I've never met these people . . ." she began to repeat.

"Okay. I'll be back early," and he turned and went. He passed the kids' room, then into the outer hall for his coat. That damn winter coat! he thought. Half the Humanities Division wore them this winter. Sheepskin-lined, turned collar, loops instead of buttonholes, suit-jacket length. It embarrassed him now, and he promised again to buy himself the sort of coat he felt right in next time around.

Coats, he thought. He'd admitted just once, to his wife, the sort of coat he wanted. Black leather, belted, all the way below the knees. *Gestapo casual,* his wife had said, and Hackbarth had filed it away, never to speak of it again. I'll never get my coat, he thought.

"I thought you were leaving," his wife said from the living room.

"I am," he said, opening the front door. "Move out smartly," he whispered, and on the porch, feeling the bitter wind, was glad for the sheepskin lining. The steps were tricky, iced. In winter, in Bavaria, on the drill field for bayonet practice, they stood in a huge circle, facing inward to the noncom in charge; on command, they screamed, *Kill!,* and their breath showed in plumes, and beneath their feet, the snow packed into a glistening crust.

"Hah!" Hackbarth snarled in his driveway, lunging, long thrust-butt stroke-return, at his Dodge.

Approaching Oates's neighborhood, his professor's eye took over. " 'All made out of ticky-tacky and they all look the same,' " he sang. Indian Hills. Zenith to the dreams of the blue-collar, he thought. Indian: beginning with Arapahoe Court, the streets slid down the alphabet—"Yaqui," he read from the slip of paper in the light of the dash. Old Red Oates, lo these many years, here in the same city. But who looks at the faces of the mechanical men in green driving telephone company trucks? Hackbarth brought back Red Oates, yanked him up through the layers in his brain, the sedimentary strata of marriage, family, and three academic degrees. Fixed, he changed Oates's olive drab to deep green, stuck a pencil behind his ear, a thick book for taking orders, or whatever, in his breast pocket. He wrapped his narrow waist in a tool belt, shod him with pole-climbing boots.

Red Oates, Red Oates. Who would ever have dreamed it of you? he asked.

The sign said *Yaqui Lane*. All made out of ticky-tacky. Indian Hills, flat as the Kansas plains where they all took basic training together before shipping over. And they all looked the same: vaguely ranch-style, drapes drawn over the picture windows, not a solitary tree anywhere on the block. About half the houses had permanent gaslights out front. "Give us a break," Hackbarth said, and rejoiced when he saw there was none on Red Oates's lawn.

He had to park well beyond, the others' cars already out front, like so many lumps of rock, a cluster of shooting stars, fallen, cooled, dead. On the walk, he paused for sociological analysis.

The Oldsmobile wagon in the drive would be Oates's. Predictable. One of two ways: either the interior would be spotless, protective seatcovers, rubber mats over the rugs, a litter bag, all aiming toward that generous trade-in—or a mess, necker's knob on the steering wheel, cigarette burns in the fabric, ashtray overflowing, tools and broken toys on the floor of the back seat, trunk filled with cardboard boxes heaped with rags and old bowling shoes, two, maybe three half-bald spare tires. The former, Hackbarth concluded, since there were no mudguards, no pennant or racoon tail on the aerial, no fluffy dice, baby shoes, or plaster skeleton dangling from the rear-view mirror.

He almost wished for his class in American Studies. Wild possibility: a field trip. What we have here, ladies and gentlemen, is a category of cultural artifacts, uniquely suitable as indicators of the texture of popular taste. The slightly aged Impala convertible with the continental kit, that will be . . .

ELEMENTS OF THE 10TH MOUNTAIN INFANTRY RECONNOITER

that will be property of Sergeant first class Joseph Ragland Morrissey. Fact is, I've seen a recent picture—usual Christmas card thing, you all know them, have doubtless appeared in them—and I read this, this pathetic, underpaid attempt at a flashy façade in the platinum rinse of his wife's hair, as well as from the neatly organized information available in my memory. It was he, then Private first class Morrissey, who introduced me to my first joint of marijauna. It was, I hasten to assure you, a long time ago.

Here, the problem gets interesting. Our three remaining vehicles must be correlated with only two owners. I select out, as they say in the Peace Corps, the nondescript Plymouth across the street. It no doubt belongs to one of our Indian Hills tribesmen. The rest is elementary. The camper is Mr. Kelsey Rhodes's, formerly of the motor pool animals, now an owner of racing quarter horses. Childless, he and his wife, I am informed, range our nation, north to Wyoming, south to New Mexico, west to California, east to Illinois, following the track. Fact is, I never liked him, barely knew him, but he shared a squad room with Rumsey, and is in town, I imagine, to buy horseflesh, or sell it, and I intend to profit—I will learn, from this horse's mouth, if races are, or are not, crooked. I suspect, quite naturally, the former.

There remains only the substantial Buick, and Mr. Lloyd Rumsey. He provides a double treat, having sent back across the Atlantic for his old *fräulein,* the former Helga Pfaff of Veitshöchheim, *Landkreis* Würzburg. And he adopted their illegitimate son, whose name I can scarcely bear waiting to hear.

Any questions? Hackbarth thought of a picture he had once seen in *Life,* of an old Sioux, holding up a cartridge pouch he was alleged to have looted from the body of a dead trooper at Little Big Horn. And another, of sixty-six men between the ages of ninety-five and one hundred and ten, the survivors of the combined Union and Confederate armies. And has the 10th Mountain Infantry come to this? he wondered, sweeping the parked automobiles again. "Ichabod, Ichabod," he muttered, deliberately mocking himself. As he went up the walk, shadows moved behind the heavy draperies.

He pushed the button, and, sure enough, there were chimes. Red Oates, ah Red Oates! he thought, and adjusted his forelock a last time before the door was opened by his old best friend.

Through the first three drinks, it was brutal. They sat against the three walls of the living room, without even the mitigating grace of music, though there was an enormous hi-fi and stereo record player between Rumsey and his wife —*home entertainment center,* Hackbarth thought, all but grinding his teeth at the monstrosity of a cabinet. After excusing his wife's absence—"under the weather . . . the kids . . . no sitters close-by . . ."—it was up to Hackbarth to prod them, one by one, to talk enough to keep himself from groveling in embarrassment on the carpet. As he did with a dull, reluctant class, he hit them at random, never allowing them the chance to perceive pattern.

Red Oates, tending bar, was, praise God, not yet totally imperceptive. Hackbarth had only to swirl the cubes in his empty glass, perhaps suck at them once or twice, before the ruddy-faced telephone company troubleshooter broke composure and asked if he'd like another. "Steady good, my man," Hackbarth said, handing him the glass. It was a short eternity before the redhead returned it, but Hackbarth had to admit he did not stint on the spirits. And it was, bless old Red, cognac, Hennessey, and Coca-Cola!

Red was the biggest shock of all. That blazing, burnished hair had gone dull, thinned, eroded in a standard male pattern. Across his forehead were now only a few whisps, and when he walked away, the bald spot in back was as big as a saucer. He smoked, instead of cigarettes, thin cigars with white plastic tips. At least he had heard of cancer.

"So how's the phone company treat you?" Hackbarth said, drinking deep to fill the space while awaiting answer. Nothing. Wait, a shrug! A draw on the cigar, a perusal of the splendidly shined toes of his shoes, a pensive chin-in-hand.

"It's a job I guess," said Red Oates.

Hackbarth drank and extended his glass. "Hit me, Red buddy. This makes my fourth, but so who's counting." He received, if not laughs, chuckles. But old Red had stayed trim. His shirt was starched, immaculate, his trouser creases razor sharp and straight as plumb lines. Had he not once been, Hackbarth reminded himself to ask later, alternate or runnerup, whatever, for battalion soldier of the month? "Looking good, Red," he said when he got his fresh drink. "How do you do it, isometrics?"

"He never eats hardly anything," Red's wife said. "I have to diet all the time." The big-boned, homely woman who hailed from some dot on the Nebraska plains—they met in a rooming house in the city, she related—at least knew her washing and ironing.

"You and me too," said Mrs. Rumsey, *née* Helga Pfaff. Amen! thought Hackbarth. She had gone downright obese since the days when the motor pool animals got her drunk enough to dance at Graf's, balancing a full glass of beer on her bosom. After speaking, her face went blank, as if somebody had pulled the plug. Periodically, she leaned across the hi-fi for cigarettes from her husband's pack, smoking like the war had just ended and she just off the boat. *Cigarette for momma,* Hackbarth was tempted to say. Mr. Rumsey's presence precluded pointed wit.

Time had stamped him, indelibly, a slugger, a breaker of teeth, cracker of ribs, smasher of noses. It had been his habit, when courting his wife at Graf's, to drag the biggest artilleryman in the room outdoors. "Close order knuckle drill!" the motor pool animals would shout, swarming after to see the blood.

He sat in an easy chair, very recently risen to foreman of a crew of city laborers. "You be surprised how much I save on gas with the city's pickup," he said. "Figure, it's eight miles, my house to the ward yard, eight miles back every night . . ." His sleeves were rolled, bursting with biceps, garish tattoos on his corded forearms, a neat black semicircle of grease-dirt rimming each fingernail. Enjoy his work? "Bunch 'a lazy niggers," Rumsey said of his subordinates. And then he did a not-too-bad Sambo dialect imitation of a black man holding his kidney, complaining of the miseries. His wife laughed hysterically, slopping cognac into her cleavage.

Hackbarth was at last able to relax his efforts. "Why didn't you wear your uniform?" he said to Joe Morrissey. "I been looking forward all week to seeing you with all those stripes."

"Nobody wears it off-duty," he said. "It's a job like any job."

"He never wears it," his wife said.

"I never figured you to get married, Joe," Hackbarth said. "The least of anyone." He had estimated Mrs. Morrissey a waitress, an usherette, maybe a grocery check-out clerk, but that seemed optimistic, what with the arithmetic required. It turned out she was a former WAF, met Joe at Fort Lewis,

Washington, where she monitored some radar screen vital to the national defense, and was, improbably, a high school graduate.

"It's no kind of life for a single man," Morrissey said, rather morosely. "You live in a damn barracks, you got nothing . . ." Hackbarth, in process of revising Mrs. Morrissey upward, to a level perhaps just a cut below girls who went to college for two years in order to qualify for stewardess training, was touched, flooded with shame of himself. Who the hell do you think you are? he asked himself.

While Mrs. Morrissey went on to detail her duties in the Women's Air Force, Hackbarth conducted a ruthless self-inventory, determined to purge himself of arrogance. *Teacher,* he sneered. He patronized his students, mocked his colleagues, seethed with contempt for his superiors. He was, he concluded, feeling better already, a man who had reached his thirty-sixth year, midpoint of life, with nothing more to show for it than a mediocre knack for verbal sarcasm and abuse coupled with a mean delight in it, lacking the courage to utter half his thoughts.

He might, on another occasion, have felt panic, but the cognac in his blood changed self-hatred that threatened to become serious to an oozy sentimentality, and he found release in pouring forth his feeling on the others, like the warm gush of a soothing fountain spewing some sweet, viscous liquid.

Suddenly, even Kelsey Rhodes looked good, with his spikes of stiff blond hair held imperfectly in place by some tonic that caught the light and infiltrated the cigarette smoke in the room with its aroma. Hackbarth longed to lean across the bowls of pretzels and nuts and chip-dip on the coffee table, put his hand on Kelsey's knee, and gently urge him to see an orthodonist before his teeth, stained a dirty spectrum from gray to yellow, visibly caked and rotting, fell out of his head. He wanted the skill to politely suggest that Rhodes clip the hair in his ears and nostrils, get something good, 4-U, 20 Mule Team Borax, to scour the grit out of his palms. He thought to ask him if cowboy boots were really more comfortable.

"How's the sport of kings?" Hackbarth said, sensing the thin film of tears coming over his eyes.

"Huh?" said Kelsey Rhodes when he realized he was addressed.

"The horses," Hackbarth said, "How are they running? You getting rich yet?" Kelsey snorted and leered, revealing the gap where a molar should have been.

"I been outta that more'n a month now," he said. "One broke a leg, other one foundered on me, the only good one I had I lost on a claim race. I been driving a cement-mixer truck now more'n a month." He pronounced it *see-meant*. Hackbarth thought of students reading the French epigraphs to Poe's stories aloud for the first time in his classes. He searched Kelsey Rhodes's face for some emotion—grief, disappointment—but finding nothing, supplied it with the memory of catching Rhodes unaware once, fifteen years before, in his squad room. Hackbarth had been sent upstairs by the first sergeant to find someone from the motor pool; he opened a door, and there stood Rhodes, looking out the window, listening to a Hank Williams record, with an expression that would have shaken the hardest heart with its raw rich, emotional need. Hackbarth had closed the door quietly, undetected, and tiptoed away. He once told his wife of it, and they both laughed.

"Red, Red," he said, getting up, clearing his throat to keep the weepy quaver out of his voice. "Mix me a double, show me your house, show me your kids sleeping," and followed Oates into the kitchen, blowing his nose fiercely into his handkerchief.

"This is terrific, terrific," he said, Red pointing out the walnut cupboards and cabinets a brother-in-law had helped him build. "Fabulous," he responded to the new oven, the futuristic wall clock, the dishwasher and clothes dryer, the intercom system that connected with basement rec room, children's bedrooms, the patio. "You mean all this is your yard?" Hackbarth said, hands cupped to his face, peering through the sweating windowpane. In the winter dark he could make out only the skeletal frame of what must have been a swing set. Red Oates informed him that his winter project this year was building a large sandbox, the kind with an awning, for his children. "I don't know which end is up with a tool in my hand," Hackbarth said.

"Hey, Red," he said after a long pull at the fresh drink. He motioned him into the kitchen. "Buddy," he said, "do you remember the time we went to Spain on furlough? That dog picked you up in the Dancing *Colon?"* He put his hand on Red's shoulder, winked. Red nodded: he did. "That was something, huh? Remember? They'd come running the minute they saw you were an American, remember?" Red Oates smiled, just a little. "You ever tell your wife about that?" Red shook his head, dropped his eyes . . . was he embarrassed? "You never told her about all the times we had, Red?" he asked softly.

"Hell, Hack, that was before I ever met my wife. What would I want to tell her all that stuff for?" Red said lightly.

Leaning close, Hackbarth whispered. "Hey, Red. Tell me. Here you got all this, house, wife, family. You work a steady job. What do you think of it?"

"How's that?" Red said.

"I mean. You know what I mean, Red. Look, here I see

you first time in years, right? I'm wondering, see? I mean, in my mind, you know, the way I know you, what you *are,* get me? What you are in my mind, up until tonight, you're Red Oates, see? You're BAR man, third squad, defense platoon, see? All these years." Red Oates seemed to be trying to look over his shoulder, as if afraid somebody's glass would empty in his absence. "You know what I'm talking about? For example, you got a family now. Kids. How you like being a father, having kids, what do you *think about it,* Red?"

Red spoke with his head averted, as if Hackbarth's breath stank. "I don't know what you mean. You get married, you have kids. It just happens. It comes with it, right?" Hackbarth released him, lowered his head, felt as if he might, again, cry.

"What do you think of me, Red?"

"What do you mean?"

"How do I seem to you? Do I look different? Are you seeing me, I mean, me, now, the way I am, or can you still see me . . . you know, you know what I mean."

"Hell, Hack, I don't know what you're like now, I haven't seen you for . . ."

"Try, Red," Hackbarth said. "I want you to try and tell me what you think." Red said nothing. "Come . . . on . . . Red!" Hackbarth chanted like a cheerleader.

"You better ease up on the cognac, Hack," he said. "You'll be ending up in a snowbank tonight yet." Had he not known how seriously well-intentioned it was, Hackbarth would have been mortally insulted. He suppressed an instinct to tell how much liquor he could hold, remembering he was thinking of the days when he was a soldier.

Red left him there in the kitchen with all the wonderful cabinets and appliances. Hackbarth blew his nose again and wiped his eyes before joining the others. If Red Oates thought anything of it, it didn't show on his face.

But Hackbarth could not have cared either way. He had given up on them, and noted with a smirk that Mrs. Rhodes, as he entered the living room, was speaking her first words of the evening: she described to Mrs. Rumsey, in a voice high and strong enough to have carried throughout the house, the wedding of her younger sister down in Albuquerque.

Hackbarth, resolute, sat, only a little unsteady, after drawing his chair close to Joe Morrissey's end of the sofa. He wanted to talk about the army with the sergeant first class, who could still be counted on to care, since it had been his life. Sentiment, Hackbarth thought, is wasted—he let a collage pass before him, low moments in his life when he had allowed the fact that literature affected him be known to a class, to his infinite mortification.

"Have you ever run into any of our old noncoms?" he asked Morrissey.

"Are you kidding, Hack?" Joe said. "Those old cobs, the last of them probably retired five years ago."

"Couldn't be, not all of them," he said. "Dosa? Okay, Dosa was pretty long in the tooth even then. How about Cunningham, he wasn't over twenty-five, -six. You mean you been all this time in the army and you never once ran into anybody we knew then?"

"Cunningham," Morrissey said with the unconcealed condescension Hackbarth would have used on a student blind to the central image of a poem, "would be forty if you're right. If he had five years in when we knew him, then he's more'n eligible for retirement. You don't seem to get it," he said. "I retire in two years, Hack." Hackbarth was only beginning to get it.

The army, Joe Morrissey made abundantly clear to him, was a very different thing than it was when Hackbarth was a soldier. The various ranks and pay grades, the organization of battalions, regiments, whole infantry divisions, were radically changed. Did he think they still wore OD uniforms and Ike jackets? Besides, Morrissey was with the engineers, not the infantry. Hackbarth tuned out while he described the laying of a floating bridge on a maneuver the year before in subzero weather in Alaska. How the hell? Hackbarth wondered. Why the hell do they change something like an army?

"Tell you the truth," Joe said, "I been so many goddamn places, I couldn't give you the names of five men outside ourselves who were in that company."

"I could," Hackbarth said, and he would have, but Red Oates came around with drinks, for once without being asked. Mrs. Oates mentioned something about coffee and cake—was she pushing back a yawn with her fist? Hackbarth recalled how, in the post EM Club, the German waitresses stood waiting for them to leave after serving last call for alcohol.

Hackbarth listened over the edge of his glass as Lloyd Rumsey told Kelsey Rhodes of evicting a tenant from a house he owned.

"You own two houses?" Hackbarth said.

"I own three," Rumsey said.

"We own three," his wife said.

"I'm subject to own four when I find what I want, too," he added. Hackbarth rolled with the punch, adjusted, reconciled himself by calling up visions of Helga Pfaff pinching the dignity out of every paycheck her husband brought home. How else explain it? thought Hackbarth, who rented.

They spoke of money. Rumsey, the muscled entrepreneur, lectured on the fine points to observe when shopping for investment property. Red Oates, his wife's face fairly glowing, related the cut rate on AT&T available to him through the telephone company. He mentioned his credit union, and a stock club he had recently joined. "They still looking for members?" Hackbarth inquired.

"You need to be voted on, and it's up to a thou now just to initiate," Red said with the disdain Hackbarth employed to squelch queries from second-rate students seeking information about graduate study. Joe Morrissey described skill-pay, and the pension he would enjoy in two years. His wife praised free medical treatment. Kelsey Rhodes alluded to the advantage his insider's knowledge gave him when making pari-mutuel bets; the previous season, he said, he hit a daily double for eight thousand dollars one afternoon. Hackbarth prayed he lied.

"Oh we made out real good on that one," his wife said, broaching her second topic of the night. The ladies got up to serve cake and coffee. Hackbarth hastily calculated the fringe benefits of his contract, and wondered if he was really all that sure of receiving tenure.

He suffered a deep, depressing silence as they all ate, relieved only by references to calories that made him pull in his stomach and lift his chin to thwart his dewlap, but had no affect on Mrs. Rumsey, who only laughed and had seconds. When he asked for another drink, Red Oates got it with an offended attitude.

He barely finished it before there was a general standing and putting on of coats—his damn coat! The murmur and chaotic movement in the center of the room reminded him of the mad twenty minutes between first whistle and reveille.

"I don't stand reveille," Joe Morrissey was saying to him, though Hackbarth had no memory of asking any questions. "I live off post, in a house, the same as you do."

There was movement toward the door, shaking of hands —it was over! "It's hardly dark," he said, as he used to say, as everyone used to say, back then, whenever anyone suggested they pack it in and get some sleep. Now the door was open, they were clustered on the porch, gasping at the cold.

Hackbarth stood apart, paralyzed. He had never in his life hit a man in the face with his fist. Never bet on a horse race. Never been to Alaska or Japan or Panama. Never built anything with his hands. "I think this was a terrific idea," he said to Red Oates and his wife, who shivered in the open doorway. "I can't thank you enough for taking the trouble to set this all up . . ." They smiled woodenly, assured him it was nothing, a pleasure ". . . because it means a lot to me," he said. They would not notice, in the whipping wind, the emotion in his voice. The others seemed to be listening, waiting for him on the walk. "Because if I'm never anything else in my life—" He was just short of blubbering now, aware he sounded drunk, drunk enough not to care to conceal it—"if I'm never anything else," he said, "it means a great deal to me that I was a soldier once. You remember." There was silence, the wind and cold. Red's wife retreated inside as he swung the door shut; Hackbarth caught it just in time.

"Red," he said hoarsely, "remember when you nearly made soldier of the month that time?"

"What do you think I am, Hack?" he said. "That was fifteen years ago, man." Hackbarth joined the others on the walk, about to suggest they adjourn to somewhere, make a night of it.

"You know you never were for crap as a soldier," said

Sergeant first class Morrissey, the man who should know, as Hackbarth reached him. He did not reply. He went on past them, and when he hit the sidewalk, executed a smart, military left-facing movement and marched down the block to his Dodge. He heard nothing, but suspected they talked about him, as he felt when a group of students quieted at his approach.

In the morning, he promised himself, I will remember every bit of this.

He stumbled going up the front steps. On the porch, he had to pause a moment, check to be sure it was his house; on the dimly lit street, leaning out over the porch rail now to be sure, all the houses, yards, winter-bare shade trees, looked alike to Hackbarth, but it was a comforting perception. He sighed, then spat ineptly into the snow cover below.

It was his house. He turned as his wife unhooked the security chain and let him in. He must have looked more shakey than he felt just then, for she held him, supporting, all the way, through the living room, past the kids' room where a nightlight glowed in a far corner, to their bedroom. He was humming something, very faint and low as he undressed . . . *Annaliese* or *Schlafen im Bahnhof,* he was not sure.

Stepping out of his trousers, he nearly fell, but with a frantic, jogging, one-legged dance, saved his balance. Proud, Hackbarth tossed his trousers in a heap on his dresser.

"It must have been a happy reunion," his wife said.

"Those people," Hackbarth mumbled, getting into bed, "those people are the greatest people I ever knew in my life. Bar none." She said something more, but he was falling asleep.

# THE ENTOMBED MAN OF THULE

IT IS OVER, and I admit it. Yet, certainly, that is not enough. There has to be, should be, something more. More is all. More. Listen.

There is a man in the ice in Thule. No one knows who he was or how long he has been there. The glacier creeps down from the Greenland ice cap, and one day someone saw his body there, deep in the ice. Servicemen, tourists, curious and morbid, go to see him with their cameras. He cannot be clearly seen. He wears winter clothes, perhaps the skins of animals he trapped before he was trapped himself. His face is tan and his eyes are open. His arms and legs are stretched out; he looks more astonished than dead.

Now this is useless information, grotesque information, but I want to repeat it. I thought of this, of him, as I lay awake past midnight in my empty house, listening to the rain, as patient and persistent against the window near my bed as the soft tears my pretty young wife used to cry into her handkerchief while I pretended to be asleep beside her. Oh yes, she's gone: if I knew why then I might have prevented it. Suffice it to say I am capable of cruelty, not stupid enough to escape my guilt for it. But this night in December it rained when it should have snowed in this climate, and the rain froze as it fell, and I thought of the man in the ice at Thule.

I already had the facts, from LaZotte, the local television announcer, on the eleven o'clock news. Pathetic LaZotte stood at an outline map and traced the causes of this Friday night's weather. Colliding fronts of air, he said, stratas of conflicting temperature, peculiarly positioned centers of high and low pressure. He was earnest, but the tip of his pointer quivered, and he gave way to a commercial.

Poor LaZotte. My pretty wife and I used to laugh at him, together, ridiculing his pretentious solemnity as he awkwardly ticked off the day's events in the world, scoffing at his stammers and mispronunciations. Without my wife I felt pity and remorse as he came back, seated at a desk, to recap and conclude. He tries. He explains. But his eyes, set in dark hollows, are vacant with ignorance. His receding hairline fails to make him look intelligent, only harried, and the studio lights betrayed the swath of incipient beard around his small mouth. He forgot to glance at the dummy script in his hands until it was time to pencil in artificial marginalia, and the program's credits were superimposed across his deeply lined forehead.

It is thus and so in the world today, LaZotte shakily insists, and if I could have touched him I would have patted his pale cheek and said, yes, yes, I understand, it's all right now, sleep. But it did rain all Friday night, and froze as it fell. LaZotte gave warnings.

The roads are precarious, fifty thousand homes are without power (reinforcements, trucks and men, are on the way from nearby cities to repair damage), fuel, food, and shelter are available at fire stations. Live wires menace pedestrians and autos, industry is halted, police are alerted. There will be no basketball games tomorrow, testimonial luncheons and rummage sales are canceled, examinations for civil service positions are postponed. Mothers, keep your children indoors!

But my house escaped. In the morning, when I wake, grateful that I have not dreamed, or if I have, grateful that I cannot remember it, my coffee perks and my orange juice is cold. My bath is hot. My silent mercury switches break the curtained gloom, and the telephone buzzes reassuringly in my ear when I lift the receiver from its cradle. Order prevails, and I take heart.

Biweekly, my hair is trimmed, just as biweekly my wife rose early on Saturdays to keep her appointments with her psychotherapist. The barbershop is close, so I walked because the lock on the overhead garage door is frozen fast, its coat of ice going opaque with tiny networks of cracks like veins when I hammer on it with my gloved fist. The ice covers everything. Winter-stunted shrubs bend double, each twig changed to a sharp spine. Lawns ripple and reflect the sun. Tree limbs droop, and the branch of a large oak lies across the wires carrying power to my house, like a crippled leg in a sling. My neighbor's house looked as empty as mine. From my house to the road on my driveway I shuffled like a skater, afraid to pick up my feet. The road is easier, cindered and salted because our taxes are ample. Autos left out overnight are glazed, as if a bowl of clear sugar frosting had been dumped over them and allowed to harden.

Halfway down, two strands of wire had fallen across the road, and as I approached them a woman came toward me in her car. She stopped at the wires and stretched to see over her fenders, afraid. Of course they weren't live, and if they were, her tires insulated her, but until I smiled to encourage her she sat there, then smiled back, closed her eyes, and inched her car across. And I was afraid to step on them, hopped over, like a child sparing his mother's back.

In the yard of the small Episcopal church whose Sunday bell used to wake my wife and me in time to be at the drugstore before the newspapers sold out, there is a small tree, tied with a rag to a stake for support. One shrunken brown leaf remained, hanging like a jewel in its ice jacket, an insect preserved centuries in amber: my man of Thule again.

The barbershop was dark, but I made blinders of my hands and put my face close to the window. The barbers wore coats and gloves, staring dully back at me. Inside, I was snowblind for a moment. "Can I get a haircut?" I asked, because they seemed to wait for me to speak first.

"How the hell cut hair without power?" the owner said. He began to pace angrily, perhaps to keep himself warm. "The busiest day supposed to be and no damn power," he said. He has only cut my hair once. "I called and says how about a rebate on the bill this month for this, but that's a joke you know," he said. Because he blusters with confidence I didn't tell him how I like it done. He is a racing fan, a bettor, has a picture of a horse and jockey in the winner's circle at Saratoga behind his chair, and I know only the obvious (Man O'War, Eddie Arcaro, the Derby), so we had no conversation. He bets, operates pools, laughs viciously when he collects, believes in luck.

"I can give you a haircut if you don't mind the handclippers," the other barber, a young man, said. He unfolded the apron for me and pumped up the chair a notch.

"Leave your coat on," the owner said to both of us. "You freeze your wazoo off otherwise." And he left, to phone the power company again, perhaps to rage at the sky and ice for this turn in his fortune.

"I didn't use a handclippers since I was in the navy," my barber said. I know his life: his barber's license bears an unpronounceable Polish name; he is twenty-five or -six, considers his life over since he left the navy. He laments.

"You should see the forearms on those Italian barbers from using a handclippers all their life," he said. He is nostalgic over his Mediterranean cruises, played soccer in high school, wishes he could continue to play, but admits sadly that he is too far out of shape now, drinks beer and plays darts in taverns on his nights out . . . "I learned to cut hair first on a ship in the navy, you know," he said.

"I think I remember you telling me that," I said. The owner returned.

"Hold off paying the bill for a month and see how they kick," he said, "but they got no time for complaints now." He sat in his chair and smoked, flipped savagely through the pages of a tattered girlie magazine, and we spoke no more until I left.

The jaws of the clippers were cold against my neck, my barber sniffled, the shaving cream had to come from an aerosol can because the black dispenser could not now hum and ooze warm foam into his palm, and little cuttings itched in my collar because the vacuum was powerless on its hook, like a dead snake hung over a stick. I paid and tipped what I always tip and left them to nostalgia and regret, to puzzle bitterly over the twisting of chance. On the walk back to my house the wind rose, and branches began to fall.

My neighbor telephoned me from a hardware store; his house was without power. With my permission he would enter my basement and tap my electricity somehow, start his oil furnace. "I called a little before but you were out," he said. "Then I remembered you get your hair cut on Saturday."

"Every other Saturday," I said. He is a fixer, eminently practical and efficient. At ease in flannel shirts and old trousers, laced boots, he rolls and seeds his lawn, paints, repairs storm windows, cleans gutters, putties, plasters, connects. He came later while I watched from my picture window, wearing a belt with holsters and loops for his tools, trailing a heavy electrical cord, and I listened to him work in my basement. I think he distrusts me; I hire repairmen, I allowed my wife to wash our windows last spring, I have an alien look with pliers or a screwdriver in my hand, I cannot change a flat tire or start a power mower.

The branches fell all through the afternoon and into the night. For long minutes there was silence, the ring of tire chains as one of the telephone company's olive trucks passed on the road; silence again. It began with a very high-pitched creaking, almost a scream, then deepened to a grinding, a wrenching, like the bones of a giant being torn loose from the muscles, a loud popping and snapping as the branch broke loose, a rush and crackle as it fell, a crash. Silence. One fell in my drive, its sleeve of ice shattered into tiny sparkling bits, as though a chandelier had smashed on a polished ballroom floor.

My neighbor came out to survey, already seeing the thaw when he would drag the branches into piles, section them into kindling for his fireplace with the roar of his chain saw. I watched him study the straining wires to my house, shake his head doubtfully, surely cluck his tongue. I should have called someone, the telephone company, power company, to come and brace the wires, but I did nothing.

When the sun was high the ice went from white to crystal, and as it sank, shaded blue, then blackish as dusk fell. I could make the gnarled, ice-bound trunk of the large oak turn fluid by moving my eyes across an imperfection in the glass of my picture window, but this was all. I sat, I watched; my coffee perked and my house was warm. Eleven o'clock came, and there were only the headlights of cars on the road, my neighbor's windows, the groaning of heavy limbs in the wind. I would not face LaZotte again, so went to bed and slept without dreaming.

Or if I dreamed I do not remember it, but I woke suddenly, and the house was very cold. The power lines had broken, there was a pink-white glow in my window, and I was afraid. Electrocution, fire, explosion, I thought, but this passed. I sat up in my bed and cried out, "More!"

"Listen!" I cried. "LaZotte," I said, "your facts fall short; you believe no more than I do. I am too tired to lament, to hear weeping. Luck has a stone face. You will not fix me with gadgets!" I huddled under my blankets, no pretty young wife there to warm my bed. And the man of Thule? When the glacier has moved far enough toward the coast of Greenland, it will melt, and someone will bury him.

There ought to be more.

# THE SALESMAN FROM HONG KONG

I SAW HIM for the first time one early afternoon in the city of Würzburg, Germany, early in June of 1956. I was the solitary passenger in a jeep driven by a private first class from Mankato, Minnesota. We were on our way back to our company with the afternoon delivery of mail from the army post office. My driver was nineteen years old, and gradually losing his temper over the reckless and rude way Germans drove, cycled, and walked on the crowded city streets.

We entered a busy intersection, the driver from Mankato banging the clutch to the floorboards and jamming the gearshift into low, ready to dart across the open square. Just then, a German delivery boy on a bicycle ahead of us, and to our right, shot his left arm out parallel to the pavement, and without so much as a careless or impudent glance over his shoulder at us, turned left into our path. My driver was quick, the sort of young man who, in civilian life, would belong to a hot-rod club with very severe rules of road safety and courtesy.

He hit the brake, we screeched to a stop, and the delivery boy pedaled blithely away to our left, unaware how close he had come to serious harm. The driver stood up in the open jeep, shook his fist at the departing bicyclist, and screamed uselessly after him, "You damn kraut! Are you looking to die? You wanna die, kraut!"

Just then he passed us on the left. He zipped by us on a light green Vespa scooter, so close that the top of his head nearly brushed the driver's outstretched arm. He beeped the scooter's horn, at us, at anyone who might be entering the intersection from left or right, swerved to miss two young *fräuleins* who crossed the street arm in arm, and in an instant was gone, lost in the traffic. Behind us, a streetcar motorman pulled his bell cord again and again to remind us we were holding up the transport of his passengers.

"What in the *hell* was that?" said the driver from Mankato.

"A Vespa," I said.

"I know. But what was that *on* it?"

"He looked like a Chinese," I said. I knew he was. In Europe, then as now, vehicles of foreign registration were required to display a black-on-white metal tag indicating the owner's nationality, to be carried on the rear of the vehicle near the license plate. Identifying the rare ones was a little game I played, like counting cows or telephone poles as a child will do when taking a long trip by car or train through strange country.

*D*'s for *Deutschland* were everywhere on the streets of Würzburg. There were many *RF*'s (France), *O*'s (Austria) and *GB*'s (England), many *USA*'s. Like any dedicated birdwatcher, I was proud of the less frequent *E*'s (Spain), *CH*'s (Switzerland) and *S*'s (Sweden) I had spotted. On the rear of the green Vespa was the oval tag, the letters *HK*. Hong Kong. Surely it was the only one of its kind in all of western Europe. He was a long way from home.

Soldiers, particularly American soldiers, are a good market for almost anything. The farther they are from America the more they will buy. Every soldier in Germany bought one good camera, a Leica, Retina, or Rolleiflex. Many a sister and sweetheart and mother received Rosenthal china or a 400-day clock or a Hummel figurine in the mail. Shrewd men in my company made contracts with German firms to sell personalized beer mugs, greeting cards, and bawdy neckties to their barracks comrades. In Würzburg there were two men who took their discharges in Europe to remain there and sell new Fords that were delivered at dockside in New York to enlisted men and officers who had faithfully made payments for two or three years.

Where on the continent of Europe he had been before that summer, or where in the world he went when it ended, I do not know. But this Chinese had come to Bavaria to sell us suits handmade by tailors on the other side of Asia.

There were three army installations in the city of Würzburg alone, and three more in the surrounding *Landkreis,* so he was busy that summer. One day not long after I had first seen him, he simply appeared in our company area, selling. He had great success.

He was very small, not much over five feet tall. He was a perfect stage Chinaman. He would have gone well behind the counter of a hand laundry in America, smiling noncommittally, backed by shelves of laundry string-tied in brown paper wrappers, the store smelling of hot irons and steam as he demanded the tickee before he handed over the washee. He would have fit nicely in the kitchen of a Chinese restaurant in New York, dressed in chef's whites, calmly cutting pork into cubes and mixing it with vegetables. He had large white eyeballs with very dark pupils, and wore the sort of hornrimmed glasses that in America might suggest this Chinese stayed awake long into the night reading for a degree in physics. His skin was burnt orange, perhaps from the sear of the weather whipping over his scooter's windshield. His hair glistened, clean-black cropped in a Prussian cut. Possibly his masters in Hong Kong did not pay him enough to buy his own product, for he wore a regulation German leather cyclist's jacket, canvas shoes with crepe soles, the ready-to-wear shirts and slacks available in any PX or the German Woolworth's, the *Kaufhof*. He had busy, deft hands, with moon-white, efficiently trimmed fingernails.

He used psychology, this little Chinese. He arrived in our company area two days after payday, when the men were arrogantly ready to be sold. It was a Saturday, just after the weekly inspection of quarters, and the men, relaxed and confident, were leaving the barracks in search of diversion. Lulled by a glut of cash, they were ready for a pitchman's entertainment. They were free of debt, possessed lockers full of cigarettes, shoe polish, and Quartermaster laundry vouchers, and still they had money to spend. The salesman from Hong Kong undid the straps of the Vespa's saddlebags and went to work.

He showed us a portfolio of suit styles, the full-color pages bound in a plastic cover, each page with a protecting tissue paper overlay. Most of us had been in the army just long enough to detest the anonymity and uniformity of dress olive drab and fatigue green. He showed us drawings of models slimmer and handsomer than ourselves. We inquired about prices. A handsome suit, without a vest, was forty-five dollars.

"I can't afford no lump sum forty-five beans," said a motor pool mechanic, scraping lubricating grease from under his nails with a pocketknife.

"No sweat," said the little Chinese, "Only twenty-five down, the rest on payday after you get the suit." I had expected a language barrier, an accent at least.

"What's if the suit don't fit?" asked the assistant company baker.

"Guaranteed," said the Chinese. From the saddlebags came a heavy book of fabric samples. He invited us to pinch, to rub, to judge sensuously the quality of texture, the exactness of the weave. "Quality," said the little Chinese. He grinned, professionally, unremittingly, his teeth like two ranks of even, oversize sugar lumps. Like a magician, he snapped his wrist and a tapemeasure rolled free, like a snake concealed up his sleeve. I have seen him take the measure of a man in seconds, wholly, without regard for the diversity of their backgrounds. He sold us.

His receipts were printed in crabbed Chinese characters; a carbon of the original he mailed to Hong Kong bearing our statistics; the amount of the downpayment, and his authenticating signature, tiny and illegible. The first man to buy a suit, a college dropout who had played freshman football at the University of Nebraska, provided the impetus. Momentum caught us up. A small crowd gathered around the chattering, grinning, quick-handed salesman. He filled out order blanks, measured chests, shoulders, and trouser lengths.

"I ain't got my money with me," said one man. "I keep it on deposit at American Express."

"American Express checks cheerfully accepted," grinned the little Chinese, but he recorded the man's military ID card number on the back of the check anyway.

"I don't have time to talk to you now," said another. "I have to meet someone at the bowling alley."

"I'll be back tomorrow for sure," said the salesman, "or better yet I'll come up to the bowling alley if you want. Meet me at the door. I'm not allowed to go in." The army had a policy—no solicitors allowed in the barracks or any other building on post. A man in his early fifties had been barred from entering the main post gate after our first sergeant caught him selling encyclopedias to some men polishing their boots and brass late one Friday night in the latrine.

The Chinese sold better than a dozen suits the first day; I continued to watch him after I folded my receipt and tucked it into my wallet. He spent two weeks, off and on, in our company, and when the market was saturated there, simply parked his Vespa in front of the Division Artillery Headquarters orderly room down the road and went to work there. And after DivArty there was Replacement Company, Reconnaisance Company, Post Engineers, and the military police battalion that ran the small post stockade. And after that the other posts in Würzburg, the surrounding *Landkreis,* the whole of western Germany, the continent of Europe . . . but I never knew where he went later.

I never knew his name. He had no name until the suits began to arrive by mail through the APO and he came to collect for them. A man might step out of his room where once a squad of German infantry had lived, and stop the first man to pass in the corridor on his way to the latrine or the Lister bag that held our sterilized drinking water.

"How do I look? What do you think?" he might ask the passerby, raising his arms and squaring his shoulders to show himself at advantage. "What say?" The suit would run the gamut of conservative shades from very light gray to deepest black, still creased from its trip in a sturdy suitbox bearing a return address on Kowloon Road, Hong Kong.

"You been talking to Hong Kong Harry, I see," the man in the corridor might reply.

So it went: we named him. Hong Kong Harry. Hong Kong Charlie. The Hong Kong Kid. Hong. Wong. Chong. Charlie Chan, Charlie Chink, Big Tooth Charlie. The Laundryman. The Gook. Yang and Pang. Bong and Pong. In all combinations and permutations, we named him. Debt creates arrogance. Now he had to collect the final payment.

An army barracks on a late Saturday afternoon in summer is a lonely place. There are rooms full of empty, carefully made bunk beds, and it is easy to imagine the missing men are enjoying themselves exquisitely. All the locker padlocks are snapped shut. In the orderly room the charge-of-quarters dozes or reads. All the notices and duty rosters on the bulletin board are no longer news. On the second floor someone will be playing hillbilly records: *I'm in the Jailhouse Now* and *Truck Driver's Blues* and *I Dreamed Last Night I Was in Hillbilly Heaven.* Someone else will be listening to the radio: a disc jockey who prefers jazz, beamed from the Armed Forces Network station in Frankfort. There is the sound of water drumming in the latrine shower stalls. A couple of Negroes will be cackling obscenely while they shine the toes of their combat boots until they look dipped in glass. In the dayroom, ivory balls click on the pool table and there is some shouting over the ping-pong games. Someone snores on the stuffed leather couch despite the noise.

I write two letters, begin a third, but do not complete it because they all say the same thing. I look out the window to imagine the faces of girls I went to school with, and when I fail, watch the little Chinese as he waits.

The salesman arrived before noon, cutting the motor of his scooter, putting down the kickstand, removing his order book from the saddlebags, and walking over to a low stone retaining wall opposite the barracks door, to wait, washed in the sunlight. Duty over for the day, the married noncoms left the post for lunch and their wives.

"You going to chow?" one man asked another.

"Not just yet."

"What are you waiting on?"

"My man the gook is standing by. I'm gonna wait and see if he doesn't go off."

"You don't figure on paying him?"

"Damnit, he wants to sell suits, he can sweat out collecting for them too!" So the Chinese waited. He still grinned, but grimly. He said a polite hello to the married men as they left. With all deference, he asked someone to please go in the barracks and tell Mr. So-and-so that the suit salesman was outside and would like to see him please. Mr. So-and-so sent word that he had already left for town, was on furlough in Spain, or attached on temporary duty with the airborne in Munich. The Chinese waited. I watched him.

He leaned against the stone retaining wall, never removing his leather cyclist's jacket, never ceasing to grin, listening to the sounds that came out the open barracks windows. A man who owed him nothing, a personnel clerk from California, came out in trunks, spread a blanket on the grass, and after putting on dark glasses and suntan oil, fell asleep. A man who had had a tryout with the Pittsburgh Pirates as an infielder, on extra duty for missing reveille that week, came out in fatigues, carrying a brush and a bucket of whitewash to paint the stones bordering the company street and the trunks of all the trees in the company area.

He waited. A few who owed him came out in the very late afternoon, unable to sit in the barracks any longer while fresh money burned in their pockets and they thought of the beer gardens in Würzburg. He yammered at them in liquid English until they paid. A couple of men cursed him and threatened him with violence, but he grinned on, swearing he would have them court-martialed for it. Some flatly refused to pay, and in the end, came before the company commander who had received formal letters of indebtedness through channels from the office of the provost marshal. The captain gave them the choice of paying or court-martial, and if they grumbled, told them to think twice before buying suits from a Chinaman again.

They paid, and the salesman from Hong Kong moved on to virgin markets, like a missionary following the flag of an army.

I saw him once at night, in a *Gasthaus* notorious because the management cared nothing about a soldier's race. We kept to our side, the Negroes to theirs, and there were nothing more than minor scuffles when someone drank too much or asked the wrong girl to dance by mistake. The bartender was a huge woman, over sixty, called Mum by the soldiers, and popular because she would curse anyone who asked her for American whiskey. And there was a large carpeted dance floor in the middle of the barroom. The salesman was already seated at a small table on our side when I arrived, so I never knew if he hesitated over which way he should turn when choosing sides. He watched the dancers, grinned, still wearing his leather jacket and ready-made *Kaufhof* shirt and slacks, tapping the rhythms of the songs out with his heels and fingertips. He drank wine.

He never danced himself, never went to the bar, and had his glass refilled only when the waitress stopped at his table of her own accord. I think I was about to speak to him when he turned to me, and winking at a girl who rock-and-rolled on the carpet, said, "She looks good."

"What?" I said.

"She looks good." Seeing that I heard him this time, he turned back to continue watching her. I watched him, and her, and the rest of the crowd until I finished my bottle of beer, and then I left.

I learned where he stayed in Würzburg one day in early

September while riding the municipal streetcar on my way to the *Amerika Haus,* a place where soldiers could meet young German men and women of good family who spoke English with a British accent and were interested in talking to the representatives of another culture. The streetcar screeched around a corner on the rails, heading into the central city square, and for an instant, from where I stood on the rear platform, I could see into the backyard of the *Autohof* Hotel, where I once had stayed on a three-day pass. The salesman's Vespa, its black-on-white *HK* tag visible, was parked there.

The hotel's distinction was that every room bore the name of a different city in Germany. I have no idea which one the little Chinese occupied, whether it was Bremen or Bremerhaven, München or Münster, Kiel or Kaiserslautern. It was a good hotel, clean, reasonable rates, and it was interesting to have a clerk tell me the first time I went there, "I can give you your choice of Berlin or Regensburg, sir, what you like."

I saw him once more, at the end of September. I was waiting in line at the big *Kino* to buy a loge ticket to see *Der Mann Aus Laramie,* starring Jimmy Stewart. The sound track was dubbed in German, and I was curious to see if they had been able to find someone to imitate his hesitant drawl. I was dressed in my Hong Kong gray flannel suit, the only American in the queue. I had been in Germany for a year, just beginning to feel on terms with a city populated by men who wore short leather pants in all weather and smoked cigars in paper holders. I no longer felt so terribly out of my time and context merely because housewives here marketed daily with net shopping bags instead of weekly with grocery carts, or because young women failed to shave their legs and rode, dressed in their weekend finest, sidesaddle on motorbikes, or because all the young men my age wore their hair like American delinquents. By this time Persil soap meant Persil soap to me, not the analogue of Ivory Snow. Red Zuban advertisements on billboards no longer made me think of Pall Mall, famous cigarettes.

I had made progress in my German with the rolling *r* and the soft *sch*.

I waited for my ticket, and the salesman from Hong Kong passed on the street, on his scooter, shifting gears into high, his lips pulled back against the wind as he zagged around a parked Mercedes, beeping his horn at anyone who might step out from in front of it into his path.

I shouted, "Hong!" or "Wong!" or something, and if he had heard me, stopped, surely I would have learned his name. But he did not hear me, or else he had no time to stop for talk. I might this time have asked him if at night in the *Autohof* he wrote repetitious letters to his family and friends in Hong Kong, or if he tried in the dark as he lay waiting for sleep to remember the faces of girls he had known. We might have talked.

But there were three army posts in Würzburg, three more in the surrounding *Landkreis,* and to the north, the huge military installations at Frankfurt, Wiesbaden, and Kaiserslautern; he was busy. I lost sight of him in the traffic and then turned back to keep my place in line for a ticket.

# BIG OLD GOLD OLD THING

Why so pale and wan, fond lover
Prithee, why so pale?
Sir John Suckling

THE GOLDEN BOY said goodbye to Miss Bessie Mae Regis. He bent way over to let the fat black woman kiss him one, a big smacker dead on his mouth, before he left. He was always polite and nice. He just leaned over the counter in the dim, small lobby of the St. Regis Hotel to let her kiss him; she did not have to move out of her swivel chair, which would have made her breathe hard and start in sweating in the summer-heavy air. Now, the Golden Boy thought, smiling nice for her, the *one* thing makes her breathe the hardest is that old Golden Boy himself. Nobody and no thing.

"Watch where you congregate," Miss Bessie Mae Regis said. "Don't let me hear no bad talk comin' back 'bout you, gold thing." She shook her finger at him; the big diamond with the little diamonds all around it flashed—shake your damn fat finger at me, the Golden Boy thought. He thought, get mean, fat old woman, see how I leave you be! But she was smiling at him. Well, she loves me *so!* he thought.

The Golden Boy flared his eyes like any old spooked African, and said to her, "Miss Bessie Mae! Miss Bessie Mae, you make me feel so bad I'd run away and hide myself . . . *forever!"* He stretched up, a whole foot and a half taller than this richest lady friend he ever did have, even when she stood on her toes to kiss his chin.

"Oh say, yellow thing," she said, and there were tiny tears in the fat-wrinkles around her small eyes. Lord, she *be* fat! he thought, fatter and fatter, all that money . . . he let himself be hugged, looking over the top of her head to grin at himself in the mirror behind her chair. "You my onliest big old gold thing I got in my life," she said.

Free of the thick, quivering arms, he said, "How I loiter no place at all when I don't got somethin' to buy even a coke?" Miss Bessie Mae Regis, sole owner of the St. Regis Hotel, owner of all kinds of diamond rings and wrist-watches with diamonds on them, owner of all sizes of coffee cans stuffed with folded money and hid away all over the buildings she owned, snuffed away her crying to dip into the leather purse she carried in the pocket of the smock she wore draped over her rounded stomach. She came up with two crumpled dollars for him.

"My onliest onliest Golden Boy," she said, "I ain't never gone let you go, *never!"* He walked out into the sun-blazing street, rolling the dry bills in his yellow fingers. You so tough, he thought, fat old ball of a tough thing. Can't do no better than two slacks, I *may* have to do me some looking for a new home, lady. *In-deed!* He was thinking about a Miss Tiny Willis just then.

But the first thing he did was stand in front of the big window of the Dunlop Tire store to preen up some. He slipped on the wraparound green shades he wore in all weather. He polished the pointy toes of his yellow cowboy boots on the backs of his trousers, and he jiggled his arms and swayed his hips slightly to set moving the long fringe on his buckskin jacket. Six and a half feet tall, he had to break at the knees to see the crowning glory of his orange, conked hair in the reflecting plate glass. He did just one short twirl on the blistering cement to see all of himself all at once; he felt mildly pouty and bad in the stomach. The Golden Boy thought: just sometimes, living in the world is a misery—get through a winter, and another coming fast after it.

"What you needs, my main gold man," he said to his window self, "is a change *soon!* Woman get any fatter," he said, seeing rich Bessie Mae in her swivel chair, steady counting secret money and diamonds, "she gone have you carry her on your back to collect the rents." He leered at himself, and, satisfied as he felt any right at the moment to feel, he set on down the street for King Tut's Bar to hustle up some of the good talk. Now the good talk, he thought, cure you of all this life-misery near fast as any new womens.

And they were all right; they began to hoot and whistle up for him, in front of King Tut's just as soon as he was near enough to hear it.

"*Hoooo-Eeee!*" Wakefield Brown called on him. Wakefield Brown was woofing all the time now about having stayed, he *said,* with the preacher's woman while the preacher went off to the Free Baptist meeting in Chicago. "Here come that one long golden man," said Wakefield Brown.

"Say hey, Golden Boy," T. T. Sterling sang, "you look like you got somethin' heavy in you big right han'!"

"A small thing," the Golden Boy said, palming the money for a little show, "some fat lady friend give me to be good for her."

"Hey, Golden Boy," Alphonse Prince said, "you gone give us a taste?" Golden Boy looked at Alphonse Prince. He was their joke man—so dumb, ugly young man; the Golden Boy hardly had to try to cap on him.

"Now how's come you don't strut down to that Regis Hotel and work you up some money all for your own, man?" the Golden Boy said.

"Ah, man . . ." Alphonse Prince ground his shoe sole into the cinders on the walk; he was not at all tough.

"Fat lady gots money just for one big light African," Wakefield Brown said.

"Fat lady say she gone *keep* her yellow man rights close to home," T. T. Sterling said.

"Say he got *one* lady fren' now, an' thass *all* he gone have!"

"Say she don't be lettin' no golden man step away *never* from her, man!"

The Golden Boy frowned: they were nothing but signifying him—they were signifying the Golden Boy! He waved the two dollars in front of them, because he could not think what to say to cap on them. "I got to drink all lonesome," he said, "my frens' talk so bad on me." They stopped their grinning, but it was nothing to say when he'd been pure signified. He felt the heat soaking his broad shoulders and deep chest with sweat under the buckskin jacket now. His feet burned in the squeezing boots—life was a damn misery! It did not help that they stopped talking on him.

"Aw, man," Alphonse Prince said, "forget it."

"Say now, Golden Boy," T. T. Sterling said, "we know you got womens all around you."

"Say he got some ladies he don't say nothing about, too," Wakefield Brown said.

"That's straight now," the Golden Boy said, ready to lead them inside King Tut's for a little taste. "Say I got womens on this street and some is off it, I ain't the Lord, but I'm damn true a prophet!" They laughed for him, and it would have done, but he looked down the street and saw Oreon Ridgeway, with his wife and little boy, coming along. The Golden Boy held up the yellow-pink palm of his wide hand to halt his friends, and he said, "Now you looky here."

Thin old bony Althea Ridgeway that used to was Althea Mathis, with her man Oreon, who worked six days every week for a Polack in a car garage . . . and her little boy. You thin old bony old toughest smooth thing, he thought, and his big eyes flared with the memory of Althea used-to-was Mathis. Tough thing. And her little light boy child.

With long arms and legs, and big feets he'd grow to—say that Oreon Ridgeway must be a fool—be a *very* tall yellow boy someday, skin as light as new gold money in the sun. That child must be five years old by now.

"Now looky," he said, and his men caught his meaning. Cap on you all, the Golden Boy thought, even if I *do* got to be so mean! His men looked at thin Althea Ridgeway, at her little yellow boy, at her glaring, mean-faced husband. And they winked and choked up their laughs and grouped around the Golden Boy to hear it all.

When Oreon Ridgeway and his family were about ten feet away, Golden Boy crowed out, "I gots me lady frens' I don't say nothing about."

"Say he got some secret womens," Wakefield Brown said, fixing his eyes tight on Althea Ridgeway.

"Say I know he got one least ways," T. T. Sterling sang.

"Say he just thows 'em away when he done," dumb old Alphonse Prince said, understanding at last what the Golden Boy wanted of them. "Say they got to pay."

"Cause I don't never pay like some peoples," the Golden Boy signified just as they passed. Now he had nothing but signified Oreon Ridgeway something terrible, and he had capped on his men for their bad talk, and had been mean as winter, and it should have ended then.

But just as Althea Ridgeway crossed his path she raised her pretty face up off her chest, and she looked at him, and said, "Hello, Clontine."

"My name the Golden Boy," was all he could say, and even behind his opaque wraparound shades, he could not look in her eye. Like any fool, he pulled back his purplish lips to show the gold caps on his teeth, and he shrugged off the bad eye Oreon Ridgeway put on him like cold iron.

"Man can find out some things on this street," Wakefield Brown said.

"Learn him a whole lots 'a secrets here," T. T. Sterling said.

"Say what?" Alphonse said.

"It ain't never been no secret, man," the Golden Boy said.

He bought dime beers for them. His men sat on stools in the cool, darkened bar, nodding and finger-snapping to the jukebox, and getting all the stories from the night before from Andrew Coleman, the bartender in King Tut's. One of the whores saw the Golden Boy paying for beer, and she came and stood next to him, like all she had to do was check her red-bronze hair in the backbar mirror, all the while leaning against him, but she left when he would not speak.

He felt most bad about talking on poor thin Althea Ridgeway out on the street like that. She never did him anything to be so mean. Now you take, the Golden Boy thought, this Wakefield Brown, or T. T. Sterling, and even dumb, ugly, joke man Alphonse Prince—they made little babies, and those lady friends went right downtown in taxicabs and swore warrants on them with the sheriff, and they went to trials, and it proved out who made the babies, with blood tests and all, people from the welfare—they put garnishee on Wakefield and T. T. and Alphonse, and the only way to beat garnishee was quit work and sit outside King Tut's, waiting for winter to get all on top of them, no place to go. Wait on somebody with half a slack to buy you a taste, and wait, praying winter would never come, like a fool.

Not the Golden Boy. Not this old smooth legs pretty face Althea Ridgeway-was-Mathis before she married Oreon Ridgeway. No warrant, no sheriff's man looking to lock him in no slam, no garnishee. *That* was how much tough old Althea Mathis loved him so, once. And she didn't tell Oreon Ridgeway who made her baby until later, too. The Golden Boy remembered the touch, the laugh, the whispered sugar-talk he had shared with Oreon Ridgeway's wife before she was, remembered the warm of it, and he was saddened. Now wasn't a life, he thought, a biggest misery of all? Sometimes, he thought, this yellow man don't know *how* to do!

His friends jived, but he sipped his cold beer, and sighed, and listened to his buckskin creak as he shifted on the barstool. All an' every which thing, he thought, what I got even if I be the onliest Golden Boy *ever* was?

"Where you go, good golden man?" T. T. asked.

"Ain't gone give us one more taste no way?" Alphonse said.

"Say he go back to Miss Bessie Mae Regis," Wakefield Brown said. "Say he better go on home 'fore she send out for him to come."

"I might could slap you," the Golden Boy said to him, "if you wasn't so damn small. Trouble is, my man, you got a woolly mind, but you too light behind."

*"Hoo-Eee!"* T. T. sang, "Say he done *sig*-nified that man!" Wakefield Brown shut his mouth.

"Don't nobody keeps me in no place, man," the Golden Boy said. "Don't nobody makes me *pay* for no baby I made. Pay for nothing, man. They *pays* me!"

"Wished I didn't pay for no baby," Alphonse said.

"Straight talk, Alphonse," he said. "This world, my ugly man, it ain't nothing but the misery."

As he walked out the door, Wakefield Brown found his fool's tongue. "Hear," he said, "watch out old Oreon Ridgeway don't come beat you with a stick, smart gold man. Watch out keep away from my preacher's wife, bad talking gold man."

The Golden Boy turned in the doorway, framed, white-hot sun coming over his orange-conked hair, between his spread legs and fingers, there in the dark and murky dampness of the barroom. *"Hee hee!"* he laughed on them. "Yeah. *Hee, hee, hee!"* And for that instant, there in the open doorway of King Tut's Bar, he was the real and right Golden Boy, goodest old toughest old gold man, and he could live that way forever, and never ask it to stop being so mean! He felt like he could have melted winter itself.

And it lasted until he passed the Church Without Spot or Wrinkle, doing a strong, good summertime strut, and the preacher's wife, a small woman, fine brown like coffee with just a tad cream in it, was sitting on the front steps. From inside the church, he could hear the preacher leading some children in a raggedy song: *be careful little eye, what you see, be careful little ear, what you hear.*

Passing the preacher's wife, still feeling his own right feeling, the Golden Boy picked up the rhythms of their song, and he put it into his strut, put the beat into the high heels of his cowboy boots, and when he began to sing to her, the preacher's wife just lowered her eyes.

"Look out, preacher's woman, what you do, look out, preacher gal, who you see."

"I know how to look after *me,"* she said softly to him when he stopped, barely past the half-opened church door. "How you going to care for you, smart thing?"

"I come and show you sometime," he said, giving her a good eye, moving his long arms and legs enough to keep the fringes on his jacket alive, keeping them fixed in her eyes.

"Maybe I don't need it."

"If I know a Wakefield Brown," he said, "knowing I know," he nodded his head at the church door, "then I *do* know."

"How I know the truth from you?" she asked with a smile. "I don't even see you behind them eyeglasses. You talk like some fool thinks he can fly if he wants."

"Oh, I used to could fly," the Golden Boy said. "Like a big gold bird. No more I don't 'cept when I want to do new things." He was sounding very fine, and he held his body in a promising way, like he was an old yellow daddy lion who was full up now, but when he got hungry again, *hoo-ee!*

"I'll wait and see," the preacher's wife said, getting up to go, her eyes lowered again, as if she had not said what she had.

But it was not right and real. It did not feel the sure way of it. He could not even sound out a woman without thinking how Miss Bessie Mae Regis would climb him if she heard he was sounding that preacher's wife; fat and fatter Bessie Mae Regis would ask all *kind* of questions when she heard of him signifying Oreon Ridgeway on the street, too. Damn a Miss Bessie Mae! he thought.

BIG OLD GOLD OLD THING

He was sweating hard under his buckskin, and his feet burned like *the* fire, and his stomach didn't feel good with only a few dime beers. He tried to spit the raggedy taste in his mouth into the gutter. His capped teeth ached, and when he squinted against the sun it hurt behind his eyes. "Oh, I feel a misery," the Golden Boy whispered to himself.

He damned misery, damned Miss Bessie Mae Regis and her hotel and her diamonds and money hid in coffee cans, and he damned the certain winter coming that made him afraid to leave her. Damn all! thought the Golden Boy.

He went to see an old lady friend, a Miss Tiny Willis, who kept a small place where men could roll the dice out and sip at gin if the welfare didn't catch them at it. Now Miss Tiny Willis, he thought, will give a long golden man a little taste on such a day of misery.

Miss Tiny Willis, wrapped in her many-colored Japanese dress, walked to the street door with him when he left. In the hallway she pulled herself close to him, and he let himself be pulled and squeezed like that. She snuggled her head against his chest, her tan cheek pressed on the warm leather of his jacket, fringes splayed on her bare arms and shoulders.

"My so golden man," she said, "my biggest oldest thing. How I know if you *ever* come back and see me again?"

The Golden Boy answered lazily. "I always be here someplace. Don't seem I change much, do it?"

"This girl here *any* time when you come," she said. "Say you don't never leave that old hotel woman no more, but here you come to Tiny Willis' house," she said, and she squeezed all the harder against him.

"Say what?" he said. He pulled away, opened the street

door to go, but she wouldn't release him. He tensed his mouth to hide his yawn from her.

"My good thing!"

"Woman, let me go," he said, breaking free, almost running down the walk. "Go put clothes on you," he said when she came after him, "That kimono show you to the whole damn street!" He was thinking, his stomach acid-poor like some starving man's what the owner of the St. Regis Hotel would do when she heard he went and stayed the afternoon here. Miss Tiny Willis giggled, and then let him go after kissing him quick, once, on the end of his chin.

He was almost running, almost ready to stretch his legs out and cut for it, back to the St. Regis and Miss Bessie Mae, as if there was a cold wind bringing winter chasing on him. *Deputy Sheriff. Deputy Sheriff* was printed all silver and fancy on the door.

"That's him sure," the white man at the wheel said, and he and the other white man got out and came across the street to stand close on either side of the Golden Boy.

"Are you Clontine Robinson?" one said. The two white men wore felt hats and sorry clothes, and they looked like each other so much he could not tell if it was the driver or the other white man who spoke.

"Look at him, it's gotta be him," the other white man said, and this one grinned at him, showing broken, snaggly teeth behind his pale gray lips. The Golden Boy looked down at their sweated faces. He began to close his fingers into large gold fists; it would have been so easy to knock them down and run, but he didn't. And when he knew he wouldn't fight and run, he relaxed his fingers and waited to let them do anything they wanted with him.

"I been called it some," he said to them. He didn't see them. He was seeing the sour, reeking-hot street, the sign of the St. Regis only a block away, hearing the jukebox from King Tut's around the corner.

"You know a Mrs. Bessie Matilda Regis?" one of the white men read from a paper.

"I heared that name some too."

"Then you get in the car and come with us. This is a warrant for arresting you, see? You're sworn the father of her child—"

"She got no child!" the Golden Boy said.

"She will have soon enough from what the rabbit says," the other white man said, laughing. The Golden Boy heard handcuffs rattle on the white man's belt. "Come on now," he said, not laughing anymore, putting his puffed white fingers on the Golden Boy's arm. "The county's got business with you. You'll be out in a few hours."

The misery of living had caught him, as it had caught Alphonse, Wakefield, T. T. . . . . Bessie Mae would hold him short now, hold him close to her forever, make him work a job . . . he was caught up. He let his shoulders sag, let them lead him to the car with *Deputy Sheriff* on the door. He felt like his whole, so tough life, all the way from when he understood he was big and gold and pretty, had been a bad thing leading him up to this, so he couldn't fight them, not against all he had been.

"My Golden Boy!" Miss Bessie Mae Regis, fat and fatter, cried out as she hurried toward them, half a block away. "Don't be mean on me, Golden Boy! I got your love child in me, I got to keep you mine, for my onliest gold man!" She ran a fat woman's run, and he could see, now, the line of his child in her, under that flowing smock she wore. Her fat arms stretched out as she ran, crying and begging him to forgive her for swearing out a warrant on him, she loved him so . . .

"What you doing to my man there, mister?" Miss Tiny Willis, still in her many-colored kimono dress, shouted as she came out her door to see what this fussing was.

"You got no golden man!" he yelled at the both of them, for all the street to hear. "Ain't no Golden Boy no more! Ain't no gold man, sweet tough thing for nobody no more!" The two white men moved back a step from him, like he was going to fight or run. The Golden Boy turned away from the women to get in the car, to let the white sheriff's men see they could do what they wanted and he wouldn't care. He didn't see Oreon Ridgeway come out of the alley next to Miss Tiny Willis' little place.

He didn't know Ridgeway had come for him until he turned to see if the white men understood that everything was all straight, and by then Oreon Ridgeway had reached the middle of the street and was pointing his piece at the Golden Boy.

"Smart mouth man," Oreon Ridgeway said, pointing the smoke at him. "Yellow man, what you got to say on me now? Talk on me, bitch, I kill you!" Oreon said, and fired the pistol. Miss Tiny Willis stayed on her front walk, holding her kimono dress tightly around her, as if it would keep out the noise of the gun. Bessie Mae Regis was screaming, and her scream was higher and louder, like some siren to tell the street come look quick. The white men were moving to get behind and under their car.

"Man, damn . . ." the Golden Boy started to say, but the bullet smacked him in the middle of the chest, knocked him back against the side of the sheriff's car, took his breath. The Golden Boy turned sideways and slipped to the pavement.

Oreon Ridgeway shot again, but he missed the second time. The Golden Boy heard it hit the car door just above his head. He tried to raise himself, saw Ridgeway throw his heat away and run back for his alley, but then he fell back to the pavement. His eyes closed, and then he opened them and he saw one of the white men, still hiding under the car, his sweated, stubbled face close to his, looking at him like the Golden Boy was something he had never expected to see in a natural life. He thought to explain to the white man how he had signified Oreon Ridgeway out on the street, how thin Althea Ridgeway that used to was Mathis had his boy child but never put a warrant on him, never tried to catch him up—how it was wrong to talk bad on a man that way . . . but he couldn't speak when he tried.

He rolled his head to the other side, and it seemed surely everyone was there. Miss Tiny Willis, or could be the red-haired whore from King Tut's, leaned over to look him in the face, nose twisted up like he smelled bad. He thought he heard the voice of Alphonse Prince, the joke man, say, "Man, do he be dead yet?" His chest wouldn't let him laugh. Then he couldn't see any more. Bessie Mae Regis screamed, or it could have been the siren if the white men had called an ambulance.

It was like the scream of a winter, when it comes all cold and mean on you in a single day and there is no place to go to be away from it.

# OSKAR HANSEN, JR., SPEAKS TO HIS SON

SON, LISTEN: I would have you know my father. But not the facts, the details of what I tell you. Trust my memory no more than I do (I make up what I forget). Pay no attention to the answers your aunt or uncle will give you if you think or care to ask. Forget the few photographs I keep: he is—was—not the sullen boy who glowers into the sun on the porch of the Indiana farmhouse, rigid already in rebellion against his heritage. He is not the cocky ballplayer, arms on the shoulders of two anonymous teammates, nor the slender World War I soldier, mock-serious, sitting on his bunk, pretending to play a violin for the camera. He is not (and this is how my memory's faulty eye sees him still) that aged man with too-big ears, grayed temples, false teeth that fit too-clearly uncomfortable in his mouth. The double chin, swollen paunch tell you nothing of him. Disregard the fading letters, bold block letters, black ink on yellow sheets. Those are only his words. Of my father I want you to know, not what I know, but what I feel, which is all that can ever be true. Listen, then. Better, see.

What I ask is not easy. We recede in time. Yes, your mother exists then, but she is not your mother. Then, I have never known her, and there is not the most remote chance I ever will. You? Of course not. You simply are not, and then, in this then-time, there is no faintest reason or argument or probability to imagine you will ever be. It is not easy.

Your Aunt Jane has not, I think, changed greatly. She was younger, slimmer, with fewer and shallower wrinkles at the corners of her eyes, no flecks of gray to conceal in her hair under blonde rinses, but the same cold cast of distance that keeps you from kissing her until you are told was already in her blue eyes. Then, as now, she smoked cigarettes incessantly, the ashes falling unnoticed to smear her skirt or burn a rug. Her children, your cousins, were, of course, only babies then. I pass over her husband; I know no more of him than you do (pictures, a smiling man in a blue uniform)—I know only his facts, feel nothing.

As now, she was very often present, yet not of or in our lives. She did not talk to us (myself, Arn, our mother) so much as she commented, wisely or sarcastically, on what we said. She has always been very helpful to everyone. I suspect, and it is only suspicion, that she understands better than anyone, now and then, that if only she would allow herself to come close to us, touch, she would tell me things about my father that would dissipate and destroy all I feel, all I mean to share with you now. She may have loved him more than even I, but her life has taught her prudence, caution, a fear dissembled in detachment.

She was the same. She blows cigarette smoke up and away from herself, in a stream, tilting back her head and rolling her eyes toward the ceiling, in a way that makes me feel the tangled complexities and absurdities of meaning in experience that will always be beyond my innocent interest and grasp. Jane, then, was only younger. She would not tell us if she could.

Your Uncle Arn, who bursts now into your life only two or three times a year, laden with expensive gifts, a cynical and vigorous humor, a contempt for me he is too unsubtle to hide even from you, was then a very young man. Forgive him, for he is affluent, if not rich, and childless. Then: he is tall and quite handsome; he wears old military uniforms with the chevrons removed, leers unashamedly at any woman, goes off evenings to swill beer with friends I never meet. He reveres no authority, values his future in dollars. He knows (and sometimes recites for me) an unlimited store of dirty stories, and when he steps outside, invariably clears his throat with loud, exaggerated noises, and spits viciously into the nearest gutter or bush.

I never (then as now) presume to question or doubt him, and have not lost this awe. I remember: when Arn—your Uncle Arn—rises from a chair, wherever he sits, he stands straight, rotates his broad shoulders briefly, lifts his chin to stretch the muscles of his corded neck, then reaches casually down to his crotch to adjust the hang of his penis in his shorts. This is always, this half-conscious prodding of his sex, and for me, then, it is the most magnificently masculine gesture I have ever seen. Timidly, unbelieving, I swear myself to emulate him in some distant adolescent future, and of course I never do.

Do not ask your uncle. He has lost himself in becoming what he is. He could not tell you if he would.

And our mother, Jane's, Arn's, mine. Do you remember your grandmother? I thought not. She would not have helped us. She is somehow less real than he, my father, to me. Yet hers was the presence, in the world of facts, that persists through all that time, and beyond it. Had I been denied her, as I was my father, I might care to unravel her meaning for myself, for you. Her voice comes to me, strident and angry. I see the set of her teeth, edge on edge, at the mention of his name. I hear her, frantic, pained, over long-distance wires as she tries to call me back from that pointless flight with my father. I feel the cut of her shriek as she lunges from behind a locked door to claw at him, the day he returned me. She is lost in the scuffle in that hallway, when your uncle struck his father. She is another story.

Now my father. It is not easy. Particular to general, general to particular, what difference does it make? I have facts, but must qualify them. Like the photos, the old letters, they do not suffice. I shall lie when I have to.

Example: his name was Oskar, like me, like you. But he never used it, was never called upon to answer to it in my hearing. He must have hated this foreign, anachronistic identity more than you or I can pretend to. I can muster insistence, be proud of it, but he neither could nor would. He was called Buck. Buck Hansen.

Always, he signed himself Buck (strong, black block letters—as in the letters on yellow paper). Somewhere on the backseat of that huge Chrysler, among the rest of the salvage he carried when he fled, was a long box of his business cards. I filled my pockets with them ("Help yourself," he said, "twenty-five years up the spout"), pretended they were playing cards, shuffled them, made broad fans of them until my small hands could hold no more, read them over and over again to abate the boredom of our long hours on the highway. I traced the embossed letters, my eyes closed, or during the long night on the Pennsylvania Turnpike, with the pads of my fingertips: *Hansen Engineering Company. Engineering Sales and Consulting. St. Paul, Minn.* Two telephone numbers, home and office. In the lower right-hand corner: *Buck Hansen.*

Also on the Chrysler's cavernous backseat, his latest edition of the *Engineer's Handbook*. I read the columns of logarithms until my eyes dizzied me. On the flyleaf, those black letters, *Buck Hansen, 1945.* He carried a small, needle-sharp pocketknife, to clean his nails, remove the metal slivers that worked out of his fingers (embedded years before my birth, when he worked a lathe in a machine shop), or turn small screws in delicate mechanisms. Its silver panels were engraved, *Buck,* on both sides. His tie clip was made to order, *Buck* in flowing letters, flat and shiny against the wide, bright-colored neckties men wore that summer of 1946. His cuff links were *BH* monograms, of heavy-gauge stainless steel. On the back of his wristwatch (my sole inheritance: the Masonic symbols, until I bought a new band, caused strangers to approach me, say, "Hello, Hiram," or ask, "Where were you hit on the head?" taking me for their lodge brother) he had scratched *Buck* with the point of his knife. There, do you see? He was Buck Hansen.

I remember: in the Chicago suburb where we first hid, where he paused to decide our line of flight, the man he saw to beg money (my father had trained him, years before, before engineers all went to college) said, edging toward refusal: "The smart cookies made their piles while it lasted. It was one swell hell of a war, Buck." My father nodded emphatically, knowing he could expect nothing.

On Long Island, in Mineola, when at last we reached the end, where he thought to find another chance, another life, before she knew he was broke, Lillie Broadfoot (she would have been his third wife) comforted him. He held her hand, fingers interlaced tightly, as if it were a final lifeline. She stroked his forehead with her long, white fingers, nails scarlet, saying, "Buck honey, you look so tired, I swear!" He could only sigh by then, not yet aware it was already over.

On his brother's farm (my Uncle Thurston, your great-uncle) outside Goshen, Indiana, where we rested before our big push east, where he grew up, even there he was Buck Hansen. His brother (I wish I could imitate the thickness and richness of his Swedish accent for you!) said to him, "I almost forgot you don't like being called your name, not since a kid, ain't that right." My father grinned, shaking his older brother's hand, perhaps grateful for that kindness, since there would be no others.

But names don't matter. Understand from this that even to know his name, this fact, is to know nothing of him. I am named for him (as you for me, and for him), but he seldom called me *Oskar*. Never in his letters. See how little the fact of our name can mean?

Others (just as meaningless). Born: 1896, Goshen, Indiana (this makes him forty-nine this summer, which is all I know of him). Professions: farm boy, machine shop clean-up boy, machinist (tool and die maker), tool designer, design engineer, machine tool salesman and engineering consultant. Military Service: U.S. Army, 1918–1919, Fort Sill, Oklahoma. Married: Anne (née Tanberg, 1919, Chicago, Illinois; Children: daughter Jane, born 1921, son Arn, born 1925, son Oskar, Jr., born 1937; Divorced, 1944, Milwaukee, Wisconsin; Remarried, Irene (née Peterson), 1944, Minneapolis, Minnesota, deceased 1947. Politics: Republican. Hobbies, Skills, and Interests: musician (semiprofessional), piano, violin, banjo, guitar, spoons, hambones; baseball (semiprofessional), first baseman and outfielder; general mechanics (professional competence); good and plentiful food and drink; women. Unusual Experiences: kidnapped youngest son, June, 1946, returned son to mother, August, 1946, no formal charges filed.

So much for facts.

Now, closer.

He was a big man. No, no bigger than I, not as big as

Arn. But my father had . . . he was a big man. In my memory's eye he towers, always, over me. I stand, only a shadow of his substance, my head back to look up at the steep wall of his chest and stomach. He is always stooping to speak or listen to me, reaching down with arms big and solid enough for me to climb like trees; he stands against the sun, half eclipses it, throwing me into a perpetual shade that somehow both warms and obliterates me. My father stretches up on the horizon of my past, the sole durable feature outcropping in that dim landscape.

I remember: his hands. Yes, much like mine, but his fingers were not so slender, and his skin was a fine shade darker, the hair above his knuckles and on the backs darker and thicker. On his right hand the first and second fingers were stained above the first joint by years of smoking. Even the nails were a rich orange-brown. "See what it gets you?" he said when I asked. "Learn from your old man and don't ever start." When his hand was close, on my shoulder or touching my hair, my cheek, I could always smell the faint, delicious odor of tobacco.

He wore two rings, the gold Masonic symbol, set against dark red onyx, on his right hand, and a large diamond in a plain silver setting on his left, in place of a wedding band (my mother continued to wear hers to her death, saying it was so tight it would have to be sawed off, and that was too much trouble—it is in her grave now). He seldom spoke of the Masons, but the diamond was an investment, a resource to pawn if the day ever came; he had lived long enough to value even absurd preparations for disasters.

We stopped once, somewhere in Ohio, to eat, refuel the Chrysler, and make long-distance telephone calls. A number was busy (I do not remember if it was Lilly Broadfoot's beauty parlor on Long Island or the sanitarium in Minneapolis where Irene, his second wife, was dying very slowly of an embolism). He stepped from the outdoor booth, took my hand in his (the cup of his palm swallows my fist) and led me into a small jeweler's shop.

"Can you give this a quick clean?" he said to the jeweler; he twisted the ring off, held it under the man's nose. Like a brilliant drop of clear water on my father's finger, it seemed larger and heavier in the pale, delicate hands of the jeweler. Wearing sleeve garters to keep his crisp white cuffs out of his work, the jeweler slipped his glass into his eye and examined the ring.

"That's quite a stone you have there," he said.

"It'll do for something to hock on a cold day," my father said. "It's got a nigger in it you'll see if you look close."

"Ah," the jeweler said, nodding and removing his glass when he spotted the flaw deep in the gem, a fourth as big as a grain of pepper. "I'll give it a scrub." He went to the back of his shop to scour it under a faucet.

My father winks at me, bends over to whisper in my ear (I see him now, looming enormous near the ceiling—the shop's walls seem to bend with him!). "That'll give him something to talk to the old coots at the general store about," he says softly under the noise of the running water. The corner of his mouth smiles, showing the gleam of a fleck of gold filling between two teeth, and he winks again to be sure I understand. This is secret to ourselves, the two of us.

In our private knowledge, I expand, straighten, puff with glory of sharing with him. The jeweler returns, drying the ring in his handkerchief. My father gives him a quarter (it smacks sharply on the counter top). He slips it on his finger, deft as a parlor magician, then straightens his arm, spreads his fingers out, and admires his ring. The silver setting catches the sunlight from the display window. "Think that'll get us in some of the best places now, big boy?" he says to me. The jeweler laughs for him. "Now let's us go see if Ma Bell is still on the job," he says, and we leave, the jeweler turning back to his crowded bench.

My hand inside his again, we went to telephone; the pale jeweler, his exotic glass, his elastic sleeve garters, the puzzle of wheels, springs, screws on his bench, the dozen-or-more wristwatches, tagged and hanging from wooden pegs, the displays of bands and bracelets and pins—they remain with me, of me, surrounding and subordinate to my father, with whom I now share some essential and exquisite wisdom of the manner and being of small-town Ohio jewelers and jewelry shops. The wisdom is part of us, me, and I of it, all in the presence in memory of my father.

Do you see?

His hands. They transmit a power to me I can never know in myself. We are on the farm outside Goshen. My father's voice breaks my reverie. (Am I thinking momentarily of my mother, brother, sister? Are they somewhere now on the highway south of Milwaukee? Contacting police? Will the farm be rushed in the night, or in the next minute?) "You need your ears lowered there, sonny," he says. My Uncle Thurston says the barber's only minutes away. "The hell you say," my father says. "What's he need a barber when his father's on the job? You dig out the old man's tools and I'll show you barbering plain and fancy. Unless you hocked it to get past a bad winter."

"We don't throw nothing away around here, Buck," his brother says. The box of barber's tools are found by Thurston's wife, my Aunt Marie. (My father has told me that when his father learned Thurston was going to marry her, he said he felt grateful: though she was not Swedish she did look Swedish—she is a grim woman, does not approve of divorced people, speaks little to us, fears her husband will lend his brother money, is busy in kitchen, yard, and vegetable garden. I have little of her.)

"Will you look at this," my father says. I sit on a chair, atop a volume of Rand McNally, a picture album and scrapbook, and a Swedish Bible with hard leather covers, locked shut with a brass clasp. My father ties a patched bedsheet (nothing is thrown away) around my neck, flowing to the floor, my hands folded tightly in my lap—somehow I know this is important. As he snugs the knot and runs his finger around my throat to smooth the cloth, I smell the fragrance of his Pall Malls. "Man could work his way across the country with half this," my father says.

The box is wooden, painted black, made by my grandfather. ("He was some old country Swede cocker like you'll never know," my father said.) There are two clippers, the steel dull-finished, handles curved gracefully to fit the hand. Several of the long, needle-nosed scissors; my father put his fingers in the loops at the end of the handle and snaps the air crisply; one has short and blunt blades, with ragged teeth, for thinning. The hard-rubber comb tapers to the width of a rat's tail, the teeth so fine I can barely see light through them when I hold it up in front of me. There is a whisk and two shaving brushes, two crockery mugs, and in a separate case with an inlaid lid, two straight razors. Beneath it all lies a leather strop, dried, cracked, useless now.

"I'll be damned," my father says. "You remember him in front of the mirror every Saturday morning, Thurston? Rain or shine, cold enough to freeze your fanny blue, face all lathered up, shaved his face so close it glowed like an apple."

"I do," his brother says.

"Hard-headed square-head Swede sonofabitch'd do anything to hold two bits out on the barber—remember how the farmers lined up in town on Saturday morn . . ." he begins to say.

"Don't be cussing your Pa in front of your own boy, Buck," his brother says. His wife leaves the kitchen; she will not abide such words.

"Agh," is all my father says, snapping the long scissors next to his ear, as if to get the feel of their trueness. "Watch this," he says, and reaches out with his free hand to set my head at the proper angle for him to work.

His hand descends, fingers spread, over the top of my head, grips me at the temples and base of skull, his palm over my crown. I feel pressure, and with his wrist he cocks my head to give himself the best view. The pressure releases . . . with the comb he raises tufts of my hair, the scissors clicks in my ear, the strong flutter of his fingers visible in the corner of my eye . . . my hair falls in swatches to my shoulders, slides down to rest in the bowl formed by the bedsheet in my lap. "Like downtown," he says to his brother.

But I am still feeling the shape and pressure of his fingers—I thrill with the quivering awareness that his hand is strong enough to crush my head like an eggshell if he wished to, and with the sure faith that nothing on earth could make him do it. Because he is my father, and loves me.

Hair in my lap is a small heap. His sleeves are rolled back to his elbows; when he stands back to inspect his work, I see the blue tattoo of a woman's head on his thick forearm (it is some sort of Miss Liberty, found on the arms of many veterans of the first war, I am told). His fingers rest gently on my throat, where my blood pulses close to the skin, as he guides the heavy clippers now, cold against my skin, at my nape. Again the long scissors, and he takes hold of my jaw to turn my head sideways to him, trimming near my ear; again I exult in the tactile promise of his implicit power.

"Tell me now I can't cut hair," he says to his brother.

"I'll grant you that okay," Uncle Thurston says. The whisk dusts my neck, ears, forehead. Is there any witch hazel in the house? he wants to know. Of course there is, Aunt Marie shouts from the next room, and brings it. He shakes it into his cupped hand, slaps and massages it roughly into my scalp, wipes my neck and ears with it: the clean freezing of my skin makes me tremble.

"El finishing touch, as they say in Spain," he says. My hair is slicked forward over my brow, witch hazel fumes filling my nostrils, eyes watering slightly. He stands back, squinting, comb in hand, to sight the precise engineer's line that will be my part. "That'll be two bits, never mind the tip, I'm a relative," he says, holding the concave shaving mirror up for me to see.

In the mirror, my eyes distorted, bulged, my hair glossy, pores visible, I see myself as glorious as his satisfied, posing smirk assures me I must be—because I am his, he has made me, just as he has shaped the lay of the hair on my head. "Where can a working man wash his hands, brother?" he says to Thurston.

It is this power in him I want you to feel, son, through me. Dormant, I still knew it, all during our journey that summer. And often, I saw it flash. His energies were volatile, and I never knew how they might be directed.

In Chicago, our first stop, I thought we were hurrying to reach Cal Rocker's house, to put distance between ourselves and Milwaukee before I was missed. He stopped suddenly on Clark Street. "Could you handle a meal about now?" he said.

"I thought we were going to see Cal Rocker."

"We are. Right now I want to show you the best Mexican restaurant in the world. Your mother ever make chili for you? You don't know what chili is until I show you where your old man used to get it back before the world went to hell and gone. *La Nortena,"* he said (it means, I have taken the trouble to learn, "the northerner," feminine gender). He drove again, almost recklessly now. "I can damn near taste it," he said. "I think about it and I can damn near smell it and taste it." That is what I mean here: listen, think, smell, taste—feel!

*La Nortena* was a tiny place, the windows filmed gray, the ancient floor uneven, tiles missing here and there. The linoleum counter was pitted and worn black in spots. Except for one swarthy, sideburned man who sulked in a booth, dropping cigar ashes in a coffee cup from time to time, we were the only customers. There were no napkin dispensers or sugar bowls; only salt, pepper, and clear glass bottles of chili-steeped water, plugged with the same sort of sprinkling spout my mother used to dampen laundry before ironing. The menu was chalked in Spanish on a streaked blackboard above the back-counter. There seemed to be only one lavatory, with an arrow painted on the wall to point the way, labeled *Caballeros*. Flypaper, encrusted with its victims, dangled close to our heads from the ceiling. The counterman was very old; he snubbed his cigarette out against his apron, then tucked the snipe carefully behind his ear as my father ordered.

He spoke eagerly, rubbing his hands together, rolling his lips, probing his dentures and the soft insides of his cheeks with his tongue when he paused to consider each item.

"Chili," he said, "you're still pushing chili I hope. Two big bowls, but go easy on the hot stuff for the boy here. *Burritos?*

You have *burritos* today? Two, green chili. Two apiece is the idea. Large order of flour tortillas. You have some of the red stuff, taco sauce, besides this?"—pointing at the pepper-water on the counter "—so far so good. You like a salad? Go on, you need your greens. No salad today? *Guacamole* then. No? The hell you say. Oh, and *chalupas,* that's the ticket." The swarthy man in the booth stared out past us at the empty street.

When it was before us, steaming and pungent, my father unbuttoned his suitcoat and swept the tails back, like a pianist sitting down to a concert. He breathed deeply, once, leaned forward on the stool, and began to eat. He was a man of appetite, if you understand me.

"Dig in," he said to me, picking up his spoon. I cannot recall how much I ate of the spicy food: I watched my father most of the time, while the counterman joined the dark lounger in the booth, their soft Spanish a background to my father's loud chewing and swallowing.

He ate with gestures: in one hand, he holds a hot *burrito,* poised over the chili bowl while he dribbles clear pepper-water over it. A quick twist of the wrist is necessary to point it toward his open, approaching mouth without spilling. His bite is enormous: where half the *burrito* had been is only a crescent-cut stump, the green chili mash, flecked with smatterings of beef, exposed. Still gripping the spoon in his other hand, his jaws and temples moving as he chews, he dabs at his lips with his knuckles. Swallowing with a thud deep in his throat, he breathes loudly through his nose as he gathers momentum for the next bite. Dipping into the chili with his spoon, he raises it, heaped high with red-brown beans, sucks it in. Without breaking the rhythm of his jaw, he ducks his head to dry the tear that forms in the corner of his eye on the shoulder of his jacket.

"Mmmmmmmm," he seems to intone as he eats, to me, to share his gusto, or to himself, to savor it. Midway, he stops, sets down his spoon, places his hands on his hips and breathes deeply in and out, like a runner preparing for a sprint. "Dig in boy," he says to me, "nobody holds back in this boarding house," and reaches for a tortilla, folds it around his extended finger, and with his chili spoon, fills the trough with *guacamole.*

"Jesus," he said to himself, shaking his head as if in disbelief when he finished. "I'll live to regret this." Paying (there was no register; the counterman lifted his apron to put the money in his pocket), he questioned the counterman about his menu. Why did they no longer serve *tostados?* Whatever became of the fat woman who made tortillas on the stone in the front window in the old days? They ought, he advised, to lay in some taco sauce; the pepper-water was murder. In the Chrysler again, he told me he had acquired his taste for Mexican food while serving at Fort Sill, Oklahoma. "Before your time," he said, "and most everyone else's for that matter."

Though I ate little, I felt as full as he. He stabbed at his dentures with his thumbnail, stifled belches with his clenched fist, lit a Pall Mall and spewed smoke out the open car window in long sighs of complete but momentary satisfaction. "Jesus!" he said.

"What's wrong?"

"Heartburn. We'll stop at a drugstore before we look up Rocker. Bromo and some Tums I'll be a new man." Like so much of his energies, he had wasted the edge of his appetite on something self-destructive, but he never ceased to believe in remedies. Yet to the drugstore, and to Cal Rocker's he lapsed into a silence of discomfort, and, I think, recrimination. Many times that summer, he told me he was trying to lose weight.

And drinking: we are in a cocktail lounge not far from Cal Rocker's home. It is called *Sans Souci,* the sign outside of multicolored neon, which is new then. For a short time, I am absorbed by the first television set I have ever seen, mounted high on the padded wall at one end of the long, imitation marble bar. It is late afternoon, the bar almost empty. I hear the sound of silverware being laid from the adjoining dining room.

My father and Cal Rocker are standing sideways between the fixed stools, at the bar. The bartender, immaculate in a tight red corduroy vest with silver buttons, listens carefully to them, as if they are important men, and their conversation contains vital secrets he can exploit if only he gets them straight. Their drinks are on the bar, their cigarette packages and lighters, and two not-quite-careless piles of coins and bills. There is more glow than real light from the concealed fixtures in the backbar. Cal Rocker is younger than my father. His hair is blond, he is shorter, slimmer, never not-smiling. He has just spoken, interjected his brief wisdom into my father's endless, emphatic address; Cal Rocker has just said that it was one swell hell of a war.

My father dominates. One foot is on the polished rail, knee cocked. His other leg supports him, hip a mound on which he rests one hand lightly. The other elbow is on the bar, fingers relaxed, Pall Mall burning, smoke curling up and over his wrist. His jacket open, thrown back, collar open, tie loose, his paunch hangs. "I hope to tell you," he says, "I paid forty thousand and better in income taxes three years running, and I've got the papers to swear to it what's more." The bartender shifts his chewing gum to the front edges of his teeth, bites hard (out of envy, regret, awe?). Cal Rocker bends at the waist in deference. *"Skol,"* my father says, and is all motion.

The shot glass is level before his lips (smoldering Pall Mall still in his stained fingers). He tips his head, only a few degrees, the glass is empty. It raps on the bar, he motions with a thumb (imitates a spout), the bartender is pouring, Cal Rocker is draining his last, ice-diluted dregs, a fresh Pall Mall is in my father's lips. The drinks are poured, the bartender invited to join, my father says, *"Skol!"*

They drink, his arm sweeps, his lighter clicks, he explodes smoke. "You goddamn bet you!" he says. I am frozen in this corner of time, where somewhere close there is the first television set in the world, the clatter of silverware being laid, a glowing light that suffuses myself and a gum-chewing bartender and a man named Calvin Rocker, this summer of 1946. At the center, orchestrating us, giving us life only as we respond to him, is my father, whose meaning (hence mine) embodies itself in Pall Mall cigarettes and shot glasses of amber whiskey (which he calls schnapps, no matter what it is) and the insanely large and meaningless amounts of money he has paid in taxes to the federal government during the recent war.

Cal Rocker gave him no money, and in the morning, sick, my father bent over the sink in our hotel room, wearing only baggy shorts and sleeveless undershirt, letting the water run cold from the tap on the back of his neck. "Never never never never again, I swear so help me Christ!" he said. I am sent out to buy Sal Hepatica to ease his misery.

What I tell you, son, is that he was what he was with affirmation. What he could not accept was that nothing was sufficient beyond its moment. And this knowledge scalded him. Still, he would not embrace it. And his anger could be both wonderful and violent. He would not submit, and that is something, after all.

We are driving: it is in a city (Milwaukee, Chicago, Hammond, Gary, Toledo, Cleveland . . . always eastward, toward Lillie Broadfoot). The Chrysler is hot, the wind from the scoop and the open windows like the warm draft from a wood stove. The radio is always on—Truman, strikes, the singing of Georgia Gibbs, Connie Haines, Jo Stafford. My father sits very still behind the wheel, the inflated rubber pad he sits on of no use in easing his sciatica if he moves. As he finishes his Pall Malls he flips them out the cracked wing. He glances occasionally into the rearview mirror (watching for Sheldon Rotter, the Jewish deadbeat chaser who has pursued him since the day he fled St. Paul? I am not to meet him until after Lillie, on Long Island). My father clears his throat, coughs sometimes so fiercely that his face reddens and he ends in deep wheezing. Then there is the heat again, the radio, the click of his lighter, until whatever is happening inside him has grown too strong to hold in any longer.

Someone passes him too quickly or too close, cuts into our lane, brakes abruptly, stalls when the light is green. My father erupts.

"Ugly Bohunk sonofabitch!" he screams. "Black boogie bastard!" "You damn Kike-looking Yid Heeb!" he bellows into the the close heat. "Stupid cunt, if you can't drive, park!" he roars into the face of a mild-looking woman with blue-tinted hair as she pulls her prewar Lincoln alongside. "Get to goddamn hell out of my way!" he shrieks at the back ends of Hudsons and Packards and Buicks.

We pass through the cities, heading east, and my father curses them horribly as his hope gives way to despair and the frustrations of the instant. Leaving Goshen, we pass a dull-faced farm boy, slouched on a tractor that hogs the center-line and leaves clods of dirt in its path. "Draft-dodging, tax-dodging goddamn farmer Dutchman!" my father brands him as we pass, leaning across the seat to yell out the window. The farm boy does not even blink, high on his tractor, but I recoil into the far corner of the seat, face burning, terrified, not of my father or his words, but of the fear that makes him hate so quickly and easily. I wish to fade, dissolve into the humid, sticky air, because I do not want to live in so horrible a world. "You don't want to go around repeating everything I say, you know," he said to me.

He believed in force (I do not, only, I fear, because I find so little in myself).

"What the hell," he says to Cal Rocker and an attentive bartender. "Selling is physical when we get right down to it, right? I'm serious. Ask yourself, Cal, how do you sell a man? I'll tell you, you damn well sell him when and if you overpower him, that's when. Look at yourself, ask yourself. You sell, and you sell because when you walk in on a man you're bigger than he is. And Buck Hansen does it the same way, and I've sold some in my day I hope to tell you. You walk in on him and he gets up and you bull in on him. You speak louder and deeper and clearer than he does, and you grab his hand and wrench hell out of it. I'm talking psychology now. No matter if he's five inches taller and fifty pounds heavier, you overpower him. You make him know you can kick his keester up between his shoulder blades if it suits you. You make him know it because you make yourself know it!" He jabs with his orange-brown fingertip; the bartender lowers his eyes, overpowered.

In the desk room of the Mineola Municipal Police Station, I saw him fight, in August of 1946.

They have removed the handcuffs from Ben, Lillie's

brother. He is emptying his pockets before being led to a cell (Lillie waits outside, still weeping, covering her blackened and swelling eyes with a wet washcloth, in the Chrysler). My father is only beginning to understand the situation. He holds me loosely by the hand. An officer with a clipboard lists Ben's possessions.

"You ain't keeping me here overnight, are you?" Ben says.

"We'll see," says the police office. I have never been in a police station before.

"I guess you know to keep away from Lil," my father says.

"You can tell my bitch of a sister for me . . ." Ben says before my father reaches him.

It was not much of a fight. They grappled, separated, swung wildly at each other, their punches missing or glancing off, and then the policeman stopped it. He aimed at Ben's head with his club, missed, and broke his collarbone. He swung a second time as Ben was falling, missed again, and broke the fourth finger on my father's right hand, shattering the second joint. I think I did not move; it seemed to me to be safe there so long as I did not move.

"Goddamnit, Buck," Ben said, unable to get up.

"Get up, I'll clean your damn clock," my father said. He held his broken finger, raised it to his mouth to blow gently on it.

"Now you don't want to start anything," the police officer said. He kept the club ready, trembling.

"When I hear that kind of talk I want action," my father said.

I never feared him. His violence terrified me because I had never known it existed before, but with him, I felt protected by it, even if the world would no longer be safe for me to move in again (in Milwaukee, the night he returned me to my mother, he neither defended himself nor retaliated when Arn struck him).

My Uncle Thurston boarded a riding horse on his farm, son—yes, while we were there. It was a big horse, a buckskin, with a long head, panels of big yellow teeth, eyes that rolled madly when we approached his stall. He stamped nervously, yanked sharply on his halter rope, twisted his neck to glare at us when we came around behind him. My father edged into the stall next to him, but I stopped, afraid of being kicked and bitten. "Come on," he said, "I'll show you how we tell his age by his teeth."

"I don't want to."

"He's just as scared of you as you are of him."

"He'll squeeze me against the wall," I said.

"The hell he will," my father said. He put both hands on the buckskin and pushed. "Get on over!" he said, and raising his hand, smacked the horse on the fat of his rump; it sounded like a gunshot, and the buckskin seemed to buckle under it. The horse snorted, slid back his ears, but moved. "Yagh!" my father commanded, and moved him to the other side of the stall, and I walked in beside my father, and we examined the buckskin's mouth to determine his age. What should I fear with him next to me, holding the horse's head still, pulling back the thick black lip?

But all this is nothing, son, unless you know the love. This, and that he could delight me (playing an ancient banjo at the farm: "Here's a hot Eddie Peabody number, sonny.") and shame me (begging Lillie Broadfoot to say it was not true, that she did have money—ask your Uncle Arn, ask Jane, they will tell you of shame). They mean nothing unless there is the love. What illustration will prove this to you?

It is the middle of night, and I wake, perhaps from a bad dream I cannot remember clearly enough to put away. In the dark I do not know where I am, that this is the seldom-used room on the third floor of my uncle's farm in Indiana. I am naked except for undershorts, and though it is June, very cold. I shiver and huddle on the narrow bed, and do not hear the even breathing of my father, asleep across the room.

I remember now what he—what we have done, think of my mother, brother, sister, and begin to cry softly without wanting to. I do not want to be alone, naked and cold, do not understand why I am here in this dark and strange place. I fear nothing specific, only that there is nothing I can reach, touch, that I know, that will tell me what and why I am. I bite down on my fingers, afraid to hear my own cries, but they cannot be stopped, and I am the more terrified by them.

"Oskar?" my father says from his bed. "What's the matter?"

"I'm cold," I say when I can speak.

"Come on over here with me."

"I can't see you."

"Just get up and come to my voice. Come on, it's warm here." The bare floor is cold; I walk in the dark, only a few steps, and there is the hulk of my father in his bed, up on one elbow, holding the covers open for me like a warm cave. "Snuggle up," he says, and I hear the half-asleep quality of his voice now.

He drops the light cover over me, and I inch close to him. I lay my head in the hollow of his shoulder, and he brings his other arm across me, his hand close to my face, where I clasp his fingers with both my hands. His chest and stomach and hairy leg touch and warm me the length of my body. We say no more, and soon his breathing tells me he is asleep. I lay, gently embraced, and soak away my coldness and terror in his love. And soon I sleep, to wake on my Uncle

Thurston's farm, near Goshen, Indiana, the summer of 1946.

Do you see? He loved me. He loved me enough to steal me. And to return me. He was my father.

Listen, son.

—OSKAR HANSEN, JR., SPEAKS TO HIS SON